MYSTERY

THE BLACK BAG

MYSTERY

RICHARD LYSAGHT

WOLFHOUND PRESS

Published in 2002 by
Wolfhound Press
An imprint of Merlin Publishing
16 Upper Pembroke Street
Dublin 2
Ireland
Tel: + 353 1 6764373
Fax: + 353 1 6764368
publishing@merlin.ie
www.merlin-publishing.com

British Library Cataloguing in Publication Data
A catalogue record for this book is available from the British Library.

ISBN 0-86327-886-8

5 4 3 2 1

Typeset by Carrigboy Typesetting Services
Cover design by Pierce Design
Printed by Cox & Wyman Ltd

Dedicated to
Kathleen, who fanned the spark, to John, Avril, Nicola,
Jordan, Keith, Patrick, and Lesley.

With thanks to
Joseph Howlett, for reading it and believing in it,
to Audi, Pat Crowe, Declan O'H, poet, for encouragement
and advice; to Paul, Eamon. Tom: the green group, Al & Hank:
crossword kings, Geraldine, Catherine, Paddy D, Paddy R,
for caring, and Peter O'Neill for being a wonderful
father and a "brain".

With special thanks to
Aoife Barrett and Eilis French for making this book so
much better than it was originally, and for giving life
to what has always been my dream.

Chapter One

It was the worst year of my life, and it all started getting much, much worse on the miserable, grey, cloudy Sunday afternoon when I took Snooper, my golden-coloured cocker spaniel, for a walk up the woods. I know I should have waited for Dad, and I would have, except for two reasons. One, he had lately taken to eating the face off me.

"It's because he's off the cigarettes," Mam said, whenever I asked her about Dad's short fuse. But I knew that it couldn't be just that, as he was still going up the hill at the back of the house, to where Matt Frawley's donkeys Jaws and Slug are fenced in, and having a smoke. No, it had to be something else, something serious, because Mam knew that he was having a sly smoke and she never said a word to him; a few weeks before she would have been on his case immediately.

The other reason I didn't wait for Dad was that he was on the phone, and when he gets on the phone he takes forever to get off it, and I wanted to be back in time to watch *The Simpsons* and do some serious studying for my entrance exams for secondary school. My exams started the next day.

"Tell Dad to follow me," I said to Mam, as I slipped the lead on Snooper and made for the front door. Ruthie, my three-year-old sister, stopped me. She has a round face, curly hair, big chocolate drops for eyes, little red lips, and a tubby body – I think she must take after Mam, who is on the plumpish side and who quickly starts to look like a plum pudding when she gets fed up dieting. I take after Dad – he's shaped like a beanpole. But I haven't got his hair, which is black and wavy; I have Mam's – except mine is so long.

"I'm coming too," Ruthie said. Normally she waits for Dad; he carries her on his back when she gets tired, which usually happens as soon as she's out of sight of the house and Mam.

I had to wait while she went upstairs and got Lulu, her rag doll that she insists on bringing everywhere with her, and her doody that Mam doesn't allow her to suck, except at bedtime, but Dad does.

Halfway down the road, Ruthie started complaining that I was walking too fast, so I had to slow down, which delayed me even more. When I reached the gate that opens onto the road up to the wood, I took the lead off Snooper. I never do that until he is inside the gate, but I was in a hurry and the grey clouds overhead were starting to spit rain. Anyway, Snooper is usually pressing against the gate, eager to explore the tangle of bushes and to sniff the silver birch trees for the scents of other dogs, but not this time. This time, a rustling sound in the bushes on the far side of the road drew his attention and he turned and ran over to investigate.

Snooper never saw the car coming speeding up the hill, and I saw it too late to do anything about it. I didn't even get a chance to call Snooper back; everything just happened so fast.

There was a thudding sound, like the sound of someone thumping a pillow, and then a low whimpering whine, followed by screeching brakes. I stood frozen to the ground, staring over at where Snooper lay on his side, his chest heaving frantically, his back legs twitching. Ruthie was screaming, and then her screaming turned into a rasping sound as her breathing went all funny.

The screeching of the car brakes brought Mam and Dad out of the house, and both of them came running up the road. Dad was the first to reach us. "It's all right," he said, lifting Ruthie into his arms.

The driver of the car, a bald, chubby man with glasses and a light blue suit, rushed over to Dad with his hands outstretched. "The dog came out of nowhere. I tried to stop, but. . . ." He shook his head and sighed. Dad just nodded.

Then Mam got there and took Ruthie, who was still breathing funny, into her arms. She started patting Ruthie gently on the back and going, "Shh, shh." As Dad went over and bent down beside Snooper, I watched, praying that Snooper would somehow just get up and be okay. And for a few unbelievable seconds I thought it was going to happen. Snooper raised his head. I took a few hopeful steps towards him; then a piercing yelp split the air, and I winced and turned away.

"Easy, boy, easy," I heard Dad say softly. Then Mam said gruffly into my ear, "How did this happen, Mary?" But before I could answer, she ran over to Dad: Ruthie was struggling to breathe now.

"I think you'd better get her to Pebblestown Hospital," the driver said. "I'll bring ye." As he and Mam and Ruthie went off in the car, Dad told me to run down to the house, phone the vet and bring back a blanket.

* * *

I was in bed by the time Mam came home. In fact, I spent most of that evening in my bedroom, looking over my books for the entrance exam. Not that I could take anything in: my mind was filled with thoughts of how Ruthie was, and of Snooper. A few times I thought about going downstairs, but I didn't want to chance it in case Dad started giving out to me. As we had our tea he hadn't said a word to me about what had happened, but I noticed that he was biting and pulling at his moustache, which he always does when he's annoyed.

Sometime after ten, Mam arrived home, without Ruthie.

"They're keeping her in for the night. They said there's nothing to worry about, all she had was a panic attack. They're only keeping her as a precaution," I heard Mam say as I tiptoed out onto the landing and down two steps of the stairs.

"Just as well," Dad said. "Snooper is dead."

"Oh no!" Mam groaned, and started making that tch-tch sound with her lips. "Snooper was the only thing she talked about at the hospital."

I moved down another step and the weight of my foot made it creak.

"Is that you, Mary?" Mam called out. I thought about going back to my room and saying nothing, and I would have done, only Dad shouted: "Answer your mother!"

I quickly went down the rest of the steps, stopping at the newel post to ask in a shaky voice how Ruthie was. Dad was sitting over at the table, and even though he had his back to me I could tell that he was angry.

"She's fine. They'll be letting her home tomorrow."

"No thanks to you," Dad said, turning and scowling at me. "Why in God's name you didn't keep the lead on the dog I'll never know, and it's not from the want of being told. Why didn't you wait for me? Didn't I warn you about going up through the woods on your own? I think they must be giving you lessons on how to be stupid, in that school that you're going to."

"I just didn't think. I was. . . ." My voice started shaking and I felt tears creep into my eyes.

"Didn't think. Ahh!" Dad shook his head. "That's just great. Didn't think. What in heaven's name was there to think about?" He was almost screaming at me at this stage, and his face was getting so hot and flushed that I was sure the Brylcreem he uses to control his hair was going to start sizzling.

"Your father's right," Mam interrupted. "There's been a lot of strange characters wandering through those woods lately. You know, Joe, I saw some right shifty-looking characters walking up into the woods with Johnny Mac, the last few evenings. I wonder what the attraction is?"

I knew what Mam was at: she was trying to get Dad to calm down by diverting his attention. But Dad was having none of it.

"You wouldn't know what that oddball Johnny Mac would be up to," was all he said before turning on me again. "And another thing: if you were spending

6

more time studying, instead of going on all those school trips that cost a fortune, you might be able to think. Waste of time and money, that's what they are. I suppose you'll be at the same carry-on when you go to secondary school."

"Now, Joe, don't be so hard on her. What happened could have happened to anyone. And besides," Mam said, placing her hand on his shoulder, "it could have been a lot worse. Maybe what's happened has broken a bigger cross." Mam always says that when something bad happens, and up to then Dad never had an answer to it.

That night was different. Dad stood up from his chair and said, "The only thing that those crosses are breaking, Helen, is my back." He grabbed his black duffel jacket from the back of the door. "I'm going for a walk," he said, pulling open the door.

"Joe, something will turn up – you'll see. Things will work themselves out."

Scowling, Dad looked at Mam and shook his head. "How in God's name can they, when I –" He stopped and glared at me. "You, get yourself up to bed."

I raced up the stairs and into my room. As I lay in bed listening to the muffled sound of their voices downstairs, I started to feel really annoyed with Dad. It just wasn't fair. If he hadn't spent so long on the stupid phone and hadn't been going round in a mood all the time, I would have waited for him and everything would have been all right. It was all his fault, I told myself; but I knew it wasn't.

7

As if what had happened wasn't bad enough, I still had the problem of how to ask Dad for the money to go on the school trip to London. That was in two weeks' time, on the June Bank Holiday weekend. Anyone who was going had to have the money in by Wednesday. How could I ask Dad now, after what he had been saying? I should have asked him ages before, and I meant to, but I kept putting it off, waiting for his mood to improve. Now my only hope was to tell Mam and get her to ask him.

And this was a trip that I definitely wanted to happen. Leave here by coach on Friday evening, stay overnight in a hostel in Dublin, get the boat to Holyhead on Saturday morning, and get the train to London from there. Then spend the weekend checking out the sights, come back Monday evening, rest all day Tuesday, go back to school on Wednesday and spend the day talking about the trip. Absolutely brilliant! Now, though, the only trip that I was likely to be going on was a trip out the back yard.

The next morning, I waited until I heard Dad going out to work before I went downstairs to have breakfast. As I sat at the table eating a bowl of cereal, Mam said to me not to take any notice of what Dad had said last night. "He has a lot on his mind at the moment, and it's making him touchy," she said, as she brought some plates over to the sink.

"What's wrong?"

"Nothing for you to be concerned about. Everything will work out fine, given time. You just concentrate on doing the best you can in your test this morning."

I hate it when Mam says things like that; it makes me feel as if I am Ruthie's age. I was going to ask Mam again what was wrong, but I decided not to push it — especially as I wanted to talk to her about the trip to London.

But as soon as I mentioned the word "trip", she flipped.

"Your father is definitely right when he says there are too many of those school trips. They must think that parents have nothing to do but go to the bank and draw out money. Do they think we're all living the lifestyle of the rich and famous?" Mam went on, and on, and on. I couldn't take any more, so I quickly ate a half-slice of toast, swallowed a mouthful of tea, kissed Mam — and the trip — goodbye, and left for school.

The tests were a breeze, which was just as well, because my head was all over the place. When I got to school, I started thinking about what was going to happen when Ruthie came home and found out that Snooper was dead. I kept thinking that she would take another panic attack and that Dad would really go spare.

But when Ruthie did come home she was okay — a bit sniffly, but okay. Luckily, Mam had brought her to McDonald's, before coming home, and explained to her that Snooper would have been in a lot of pain if he'd lived. This seemed to help Ruthie accept his death. And even a few days later, when I happened to say something about Snooper by mistake, Ruthie didn't start bawling her head off; she just whinged for a bit – which was just as well, because Dad was giving me bull's looks.

For the next few weeks, I kept out of Dad's way as much as possible. But that didn't really help, because Mam started picking on me. She gave me grief over the state of my room, over how much – or, as she said, how little – I helped out around the house, and over watching too much telly. I was tempted to have a go at her, but I didn't because I knew that the only reason she was giving me grief was this thing with Dad. Whatever it was, it was definitely getting to her as well. So I just bit my bottom lip and endured what she said and hoped that whatever was up with Dad would sort itself out.

And that was what seemed to have happened on the Thursday evening before the June Bank Holiday weekend, when Aunt Eileen and her nightmare of a son Kevin arrived down unexpectedly from Dublin.

Chapter Two

Aunt Eileen came in kissing and hugging everyone in sight, while her eyes darted around the room taking everything in, as usual. When we'd got past the kissing, the hugging and the same old remarks about how big Ruthie and I were getting, Aunt Eileen went and sat near the window, the way she always does, so she can keep an eye on what's happening outside as well as inside. Kevin sat behind her, where he could sneer and make faces at me without his mother seeing what he was at. Mam told me to go and tell Dad that Aunt Eileen was here.

I ran out into the back yard. Dad was standing with his head bowed, his hands joined and resting on top of a fence. He looked like he was at second Mass on Sunday; all he needed was the black pinstriped suit that he'd had on him earlier in the day, when he went to town to do some business. What sort of business, neither he nor Mam would say, but I did hear them mention something about his boss. Whatever it was, it had to be important, because Mam kept on saying to Dad that it would work out fine, and then she started asking him if he was sure he didn't want her to come with him. He said he didn't, but he looked really worried. By the time he left, he had his moustache nearly eaten off his lip.

I watched him for a few minutes, while I tried to decide whether to go and tell him that Aunt Eileen was here. Even though I knew he got on well with her, I decided not to chance it, the way that his moods were. At the same time, I didn't want Mam getting on my case for not calling him. So I shouted up at Dad, but I turned my face in towards the door, so as he wouldn't hear me and Mam would. Then I went back into the house and told Mam that Dad was busy with the donkeys.

"Don't tell me he's buying and selling donkeys now. Dear God, whatever next?" Aunt Eileen said, shaking her head.

"No, no," Mam said quickly. "He's only minding them for a neighbour who's in hospital."

"Well, I should hope so, after the last fiasco with the goats. How he ever thought that he was going to make money from such a venture, I will never know. Selling goats' milk? Why, the very thought of drinking goats' milk . . . yuck!" Aunt Eileen pulled her red-painted lips apart and made one of her I-have-just-bit-into-a-hairy-lemon faces.

Mam smacked her lips together and went over to the sink and filled the kettle with water.

"Of course, to be fair," Aunt Eileen went on, "I suppose the poor man was only using the little that the dear Lord has given him. He cannot be blamed if he is not as gifted as some." She went quiet, but not for long. "You take Kevin's father, Robert: every-thing he turned his hand to was a success. Not that he was a man who used his hands a lot – no, he was noted more for using his brains. Truly a gifted man – and they say that the dear Lord takes such types when they are young. And he was taken in his prime." She gave one or two sniffles, took out a handkerchief from her purse and dabbed at non-existent tears.

"Yes . . . what a pity he was taken," Mam said, sighing. Then she turned to me with a strained look on her face and told me to set the table.

While Aunt Eileen went on talking about her husband, I set the table.

As I put a cup and saucer down in front of Kevin, he stuck his tongue out and made some remark about there being a smell of pigs off me. I looked him up and down. He looked different from the last time when he and his mother had called, about two months before, on their way to Galway for the weekend – they are always going somewhere for the weekend. This time he was wearing a shirt and tie, and his blond hair was cut tight over his ears and thick, like himself, on top of his head.

"Don't you look a lovely little boy, all dressed up in your shirt and tie," I said, and his face reddened.

"At least I haven't got a freckly nose and gacky brown hair," he said, trying to imitate my bit of a Laois accent. He aimed a kick at me, but he missed and kicked his mother. She squealed, gave him a belt on the arm and warned him to behave himself. Then she said the words that made Mam's jaw drop to the floor.

"If you don't behave yourself, I won't let you stay here for the weekend."

"Stay here for the weekend?" Mam said, in a quivery voice. Whenever Aunt Eileen called, she and Kevin only ever stayed for a few hours, and now here she was talking about spending the weekend with us. The shock was too much for Mam; her face looked like it had been in the freezer all night.

"That is, if you don't mind," Aunt Eileen said. "You see, I have been feeling really ghastly lately; I have been missing his father even more poignantly. Why his memory should be pulling at my heart-strings at this particular time, I don't honestly know; though I suppose that, when you lose a treasure like Robert, you never, ever get over it." She gave a few heartfelt sighs. Then she said, "I wouldn't be going at all, only two of my work colleagues bought me a ticket. They just sprang the surprise on me this very morning."

"Bought you a ticket?" Mam said, confused.

"Oh, yes. For Paris, if you don't mind." Aunt Eileen smiled. "Can you imagine, I am off to the romantic capital of the world." Her face took on a dreamy

14

look as she raised her hand and gently touched her blonde hair (obviously dyed) to make sure that it was still in place. If it had moved it would have been a miracle, because it was rock-stiff on her head; she had to have spent half a day blasting it with super-firm-hold hairspray, because even when she shook her head the hair remained in the one place.

"Not that I would ever again be bothered with romance," she suddenly said, getting a big redner as she copped us all looking at her. "Not after Robert." She cleared her throat and started fiddling with her handbag.

"Oh, so you're not staying here?" Mam said, her face beginning to thaw.

"Gracious, no!" Aunt Eileen dismissed the idea with a wave of her hand. "Of course, I will only go if you can mind Kevin for me. If you have anything planned for the weekend, I will simply cancel the whole thing."

"No . . . no, I have nothing planned."

"I kind of thought that," Aunt Eileen said, and then quickly added: "Sure, why would you go anywhere when you are living in the countryside, away from all the stresses of life? I sometimes feel that you don't know how lucky you are, living out in the wilds. Not that I would swap, I have to say: I am too much of a cultured person to ever survive in the wilds. I suppose I must have inherited the trait from our dearly departed father; he inclined towards the more cultured aspects of life — while you, dear

Helen, seem to have inherited our dearly departed mother's rustic tendencies."

"My God!" Mam said, banging the kettle onto the gas cooker. She turned to me and said, "Will you go and ask your father if he wants tea?"

"But he's up with the —"

"Just go and tell him that his tea's ready," Mam said, eyeballing me out of it.

"Yes, do that, Mary. I want to see the dear man before I go," Aunt Eileen chimed in as I went out the back door.

When I told Dad that his tea was ready and that Aunt Eileen was in the house (I never said anything about Kevin staying for the weekend), he said that he had seen the queen's car arriving. By the way he said it, I knew that he was in an okay mood, though his eyes and face looked like he was on a downer.

"She won't be staying long," I said, hoping to improve his mood even more.

He put his arm around my shoulders and said, "Thank God for small mercies." Then he added, "I suppose the queen is down there giving out about the state of the house, saying this should be changed and that should be thrown out?"

"No," I said. "She's talking about her dead husband Robert."

Dad looked at me and shook his head. "Mary," he said with a heavy sigh, "I told you before, her husband didn't die; he went into hiding, and he only comes out when she's not around. Do you understand?" This was Dad's idea of a joke. Not much of a joke, but at least he was going on the way that he always used to before things changed.

"Yes," I said, after I got over the shock of him making a joke.

"Good," he said, giving my shoulder a gentle squeeze. "Now that little matter is straightened out, let's go and talk to the queen."

As we walked down to the house, I told myself that everything was definitely getting back to normal, that whatever was bothering Dad had passed; otherwise he would still be in the horrors. Maybe whatever he had done in the morning, all dressed up, had solved the problem, whatever the problem was. I had myself convinced that this was what had happened, and I became even more convinced when we went inside and Dad started joking and teasing Aunt Eileen. He didn't even seem to mind when Mam mentioned that Kevin would be staying for the weekend.

At seven o'clock, Aunt Eileen said that she had to go. She got up from her chair, looked out the window and then sat back down again and let a shriek out of her. "Who in heaven's name is that creature outside on the bicycle, with a dog that looks like a pig?"

"Look at the head on him!" Kevin said, craning his neck past his mother.

Aunt Eileen gave him a belt and told him not to be so cheeky. Then she peered out the window again and said, "What an ugly-looking brute. Who is he?"

"Oh, that's Johnny Mac, your sister's fancy man," said Dad, "taking his dog for a walk."

"My sister's *what*?" Aunt Eileen said, looking wide-eyed at Mam.

"Don't take any notice of what that fellow says,"

Mam said, taking a brown paper bag out of one of the presses in the dresser and going out the door.

"She's not bringing him in here, is she?" Aunt Eileen said, looking anxiously at Dad.

"No. Johnny never comes in when he has one of his bull terriers with him. Those dogs would savage you. Why he has them so vicious, I'll never know. I suppose he must be frightened of someone breaking into his house."

"Breaking out, more like, when they'd see the cut of him," Aunt Eileen remarked, glancing out again to get a better look at Johnny Mac. "But what is he doing outside my sister's gate?" She sounded annoyed.

"Waiting for the scones that your sister makes and gives to him for his tea. He calls every evening."

"My God! My only sister has taken to feeding waifs and degenerates now," Aunt Eileen said, turning from the window.

"Ohhh," Dad said, stretching the word, "I wouldn't say that about Johnny Mac. In fact, Johnny Mac wouldn't be a bad catch at all for a widowed woman. I admit that he's a bit rough about the edges, but still. . . ."

"Joseph O'Neill!" Aunt Eileen humphed. "Have you totally lost whatever modicum of sense is in that brain of yours?"

"Oh, now, don't be so quick to judge the man. He has his own cottage less than a mile from here. Well in off the road, it is, and it's on the best part of an acre of land — though I do admit that the house itself is in need of a lick of paint and a woman's expert touch."

"Probably needs to be fumigated, like him," Aunt Eileen said, peering out the window again.

"No, no. I think a woman like yourself could do wonders with Johnny Mac's place, and with Johnny Mac himself."

"God help you, child," Aunt Eileen said, looking at me and sighing. "It's a wonder that you and little Ruthie aren't up in the Big House getting treatment." She sighed again. "For your father definitely needs treatment, a lot of treatment, but

19

unfortunately it is too late for him. And as for your mother, I dare say that she needs it as well."

"Needs what?" Mam said, coming back in.

"Oh, it doesn't matter," Aunt Eileen said, rising. "I must be going. Now you be good for your Aunt Helen and Uncle Joseph," she said to Kevin, and then she kissed and hugged us all again, including Dad, who told her that he would see what he could do about tidying Johnny Mac up for when she came back on Monday.

"Definitely a head-case," Aunt Eileen said, as she hurried out the door and into her car.

Chapter Three

I was sorry to see Aunt Eileen leave, because later that night Dad got into a mood again. I could hear him downstairs moaning and giving out to Mam, saying something about us being a charity case. Apparently Aunt Eileen had given money to Mam for keeping Kevin for the weekend, and this was getting up Dad's nose big-time. I could have sneaked out onto the landing and heard exactly what he was saying, but I couldn't be bothered. I was sick of Dad and his moods, and anyway, I was in a bit of a mood myself: my classmates were in Dublin by now, having themselves a ball, while I was stuck at home like a forgotten Cinderella. And if that wasn't the pits, I had Kevin the Horror to put up with as well. I could have screamed the house down, especially as I knew that Mam would be on my case to keep him amused and out of her hair.

I was right. The next morning, while the Horror was at the table stuffing his face and I was at the sink filling the kettle, Mam came over to me and said, "Keep an eye on him while I go and get clothes for a wash."

Keep an eye on him? I felt like telling Mam, as she went upstairs, that it was a rope that should be kept on him – around his neck – but I didn't; I just went over to the table to eat the two slices of toast that I'd left on the plate. Of course the toast was gone. No prizes for guessing who took it.

"You're funny, Kevin," Ruthie said, laughing. Kevin said nothing; the big smirk on his face said it all.

"What did you do with my toast?" I said, and his smirk got even bigger. "Where did you put it?" I looked around the table and spotted the rim of a plate underneath a tea-towel, but when I picked up the tea-towel the plate was empty. Ruthie started laughing her head off, and Kevin began hee-hee-ing out of him like a hyena.

"Come on," I said, "tell me where the toast is before it gets cold."

"Do you really want to know?" he said, delighted with himself.

"Yes," I said, and Ruthie started jumping up and down in her chair, all excited.

Kevin started hee-hee-ing again, and then he let his head fall back and opened his mouth. Ruthie clapped her hands with joy. He looked to me like a giant goldfish waiting to be fed. Then he pointed to his goldfish mouth with his finger.

I looked down at his plate, at the bit of a crust that he hadn't eaten; then I reached over, grabbed it and quickly popped it into his mouth. Kevin made a gargling sound, only much louder, and started hopping about in the chair, his face turning bright red, his eyes spilling tears down his cheeks. He was squirming about so much that he eventually fell onto the floor. Ruthie roared with laughter.

Mam roared too, but it wasn't with laughter. "What in God's name is going on?" she shouted, thundering down the stairs with an armful of bedclothes. She dropped the clothes on the floor beside the washing machine and came rushing over to the table.

Kevin was holding his throat, real dramatically, and going "Aaargggh" like a mad thing. Mam picked him up and started slapping him between the shoulder-blades. I was tempted to ask her to let me give him a few slaps as well, but the dagger looks she gave me as soon as Kevin managed to spit out the bit of toast made me forget it.

"Did it go down with your breath?" Mam said, putting her arms around him consolingly. "Here, have a drink of tea." She held the cup up to his lips and made him drink from it. "There, that's better. You're all right now, aren't you, pet?" she said, like she was talking to a baby, hugging him and stroking his mush with her fingers and kissing away the tears from his eyes. All she was short of doing was tickling him under the chin and going "Coochie-coo", but, thank God, Ruthie and I were spared that spectacle. "Will I make you some more toast?"

Kevin shook his head vigorously.

"Okay, then, you just sit down in the chair for a few minutes and take it easy," Mam said, patting him gently on the head. Then she frowned at me and said, "I thought I told you to watch him." When I didn't answer, she shook her head with temper and started banging the clothes into the washing machine.

Of course, I could have told Mam that I was too busy making his bottle to watch him, and anyway she should have known that you don't give babies toast to chew on, you give them rusks. But why bother saying it? It might upset poor Tiny Tears sitting at the table, and we wouldn't want to do that, now would we?

For the next few minutes, Kevin sat in the chair without as much as a peep out of him, but the look on his face told me that he was planning something. Ruthie kept on laughing, which didn't impress Kevin at all. He kept turning around and glaring at her bull-eyed, but she just put her hand up to her mouth and kept laughing. She must have thought that she was at the circus.

I put a slice of bread into the toaster and kept a wary eye on Kevin. He was going to do something. I became certain of it when he said in a honeyed voice, "Auntie Helen, may I have a Biro, please?"

"Oh, you want to write a letter," Mam said, opening the pine dresser's left drawer, which is her stationery department. I nearly got sick. How could Mam be so dumb as to think that Kevin wanted a Biro to write a letter? He wanted it to jab me with, more like.

Mam gave him a Biro and a writing-pad, and then went upstairs to get more clothes. As soon as she was gone, Kevin was up off the chair and over searching about in the dresser. Ruthie started screaming and pointing at him.

"Shut up, you frizzy-haired muppet," he said, sneering at her.

"Take no notice of him, Ruthie," I said, buttering a slice of toast for her. "He's mad, cuckoo."

"You're a smelly pig," Kevin said, slipping something I didn't see into the jacket pocket of his navy-blue tracksuit.

"What would you know? You're mad."

"I am not mad!" he shouted.

I smiled at him, because I knew he had lost it, and that made him worse. "I'm not mad and you're a smelly pig!" he yelled, his face blazing.

I was about to answer him, but Mam came down the stairs with more clothes. "What are you saying to Kevin?"

"Nothing."

"Don't lie to me, Mary." She put the clothes into the washing machine and then came over to the table and put her hands on Kevin's shoulders. "You don't take any notice of what that one says to you. She's getting far too big for her boots lately." I sighed and shook my head. "Mary O'Neill, will you behave yourself! Now, if you're finished having your breakfast, you can get yourself over

25

to the sink and wash those dishes while I hoover upstairs."

Kevin grinned at me as I got up from the chair. I stuck my tongue out at him, but unfortunately Mam caught me. "Mary!" she snapped. "You are really pushing it. Any more of that type of behaviour, and your father will hear about it when he gets home." She started over towards the stairs and then stopped. "Oh, and before I forget, when you're finished with the dishes you can tidy your room. You have it like a rubbish tip – everything flung around all over the place."

As I washed the dishes, Kevin started muttering out of him in a whiny voice that was supposed to be Mam's: "Wash the dishes for Mammy, and then tidy your room, you smelly pig." He tittered and then said the same thing again.

I took no notice of him; I was thinking about the girls in my class. They would be on the boat by now. I could just see them running to the front of the boat and standing on the rails doing impersonations of Leonardo Di Caprio and Kate Winslet, while I was stuck here doing a washerwoman impersonation with Dennis the Menace – who, thankfully, was keeping his big mouth shut at the moment – for company. Adding to my misery was the sun: it was blazing in through the front window, and the forecast was for a scorcher for the whole long weekend.

I thought about the poster of Leonardo's face hanging up on my bedroom wall. My mates all used to have Leonardo posters as well, but it only took about three months before they were swapping them for posters of Westlife. They slag me for still having Leonardo on my wall, but I don't care, he's gorgeous and I love him, and I'll still love him when he's forty and baldy. Anyway, maybe it was the fact that I had my hands in the water, amongst the dishes, but I could see myself in the sea with Leonardo, instead of Kate Winslet. I was giving the dream loads when the sound of Ruthie crying broke the spell.

I looked round. Kevin had an empty Biro tube stuck in his gob and

27

was spraying pearl barley at Ruthie. I picked up the wet dishcloth off the draining board and was halfway across the floor to him when he saw me. He jumped up out of the chair and ran screaming towards the front door, but the door was closed. As he frantically tried to open it, I raised my arm, and I was just about to let fly when the sound of Mam's voice stopped me.

"Je — God Almighty in heaven! Mary O'Neill, what are you doing now?"

I knew it was pointless trying to explain to her what had happened, but before I could even try she was pointing at my head. "What is that white stuff in your hair?" I ran my left hand through my hair and ended up with a handful of pearl barley.

I looked at Kevin. He started sniggering at me. I decided to let him experience what a wet dishcloth across the kisser tasted like, and shove the consequences, but Mam grabbed the cloth from my hand.

"Look at the state of the floor," she fumed. "Get a mop! . . . No, don't bother. I'm sending you both to the village to get some messages, and you can bring Ruth with ye. Now go and brush that stuff out of your hair. Honestly, Mary, I'm beginning to think that you should be going into playschool and not secondary. . . ." She never said a word to darling Kevin.

I went to my bedroom. As I brushed my hair, tied it back with a bobbin, and then put on jeans and a T-shirt, I could hear Kevin tittering downstairs and repeating what Mam had said about me going to

28

playschool. And then I heard him say, "Please, Auntie Helen, will you let me go for a ride on one of the donkeys?"

I was delighted when I heard Mam say no. Then he started sucking up to her, saying that she was his favourite auntie and other real puke-into-a-bag stuff. Mam still said no, and I was proud of her; but then, when he kept on sucking up to her, she said yes. I felt like roaring down at her that they must have all been boneheads in the school she went to, and I might have done it, too, if I'd thought Mam would listen. But all she would have done was turn on me.

I looked at the poster of Leonardo's face and sighed, and then I went downstairs and waited for Mam to brush Ruthie's hair.

Chapter Four

On the way to the shops, I had to endure Ruthie moaning that she wanted to be carried, and when I wouldn't carry her she kept dropping Lulu and her doody, and I had to go back and pick up the stupid things to stop her crying. And, just to add to my misery, I also had Kevin moaning into my ear — first about Ruthie coming to the shops with us, and then about there being no buses.

What a pain.

Eventually, he gave up moaning and started pelting me with pearl barley. I ran after him a few times, to give him a box, but I couldn't run very far because of Ruthie being with me. I was afraid that if I didn't keep hold of her hand she might run out onto the road and get hit by a car, like Snooper did. Anyway, it was too warm to be chasing after a fool. The tar on the road was bubbling in places and my T-shirt was beginning to stick to my back.

I decided to just ignore Kevin and hope that he would get more daring and come too close to me. If he did, I would catch him. I did ignore him, but it wasn't easy, as he kept spitting those things at me. And what really maddened me were the shouts of delight out of him whenever he managed to hit me on the nose, which he did a few times — a few times too many for my liking.

Eventually the heat got to him and he stopped spraying me with barley and just walked behind me — a little too far behind for me to catch him, unfortunately. He started moaning again, got tired doing that and began chirping about some secret that he knew.

"What secret?" I said, just a little bit curious.

"A secret that you don't know anything about."

"Yeah, right, Kevin. Why don't you go and stuff your secret?"

"It's about your da."

I looked at him, at the dots of perspiration across his forehead and under his eyes and nose that gave an overall sheen to his mug, and sighed. "You don't know anything about my dad."

"I do know something," he said.

"Like what?"

"Something you don't know."

Now I was more than a little curious; now I was dying to know what Kevin knew. But I couldn't let him know that, so I laughed at him and said, "Kevin Smith, there's nothing you know about my dad that I don't already know." I tightened my grip on Ruthie's hand and walked on.

"Well, if there isn't," he said, running up beside me, grinning, "then how come I heard your da saying to your ma last night that you weren't to be told?"

"Told what?" I said, and as the grin on his face grew so big that I could see his pinky top gums, I lost it. I made a dive for him, but his arm was as slippy as a wet bar of soap, and my fingers couldn't get a proper grip. He pulled away from me and ran out into the middle of the road. I took a swipe at him and got the fright of my life as I bumped into something solid. The next thing I heard was a scream and a chorus of curses ringing through the air.

"What the – what the – what do you think you're at, you thick, stupid. . . ."

It was Johnny Mac. He had appeared out of nowhere and now he was wobbling all over the road on his bike, cursing and swearing, because I had clobbered him one. I didn't know whether to shout that I was sorry or to just turn around and run.

Kevin wasn't helping things by ha-ha-ing out of himself and pointing his finger at Johnny Mac. "Look what you've done now," he said, coming over to me.

I said nothing. I didn't even belt him, and I could have, because he was standing right beside me. I was too worried about what Johnny Mac was going to do when he got his bike under control.

When Johnny Mac did manage to stop the bike, I walked slowly towards him, saying that I was very, very sorry. He stood there muttering to himself, taking no notice of me; he was too busy checking the black bag that was tied to the carrier on the back of his bike. In fact, I was sure that he was just going to cycle away and not bother with us at all. And he might have done, if it hadn't been for Kevin.

"Where's that smelly pong coming from?" Kevin said, laughing.

Immediately Johnny Mac turned, tilted his head back and glared at us; his one good eye looked each of us up and down, starting with Ruthie, who was holding on to my hand for dear life and trying to hide behind my right leg at the same time. The sight of Johnny Mac always frightened her — frightened me too, though I would never admit it to anyone. The left side of his face was all scrunched up, bloated, and over to one side, like it was trying to get away from the other side of his face. Where his left eye should have been there was just a load of lumpy red skin, though Dad said that Johnny did have a left eye and that was why he tilted his head back when he was looking at you — so that he could see out of it. He always wore black hobnailed boots that were scuffed and scarred with a million scratches, black trousers that were shiny with dirt, a short grey jacket that was fastened at the middle button and that layers of dirt were slowly turning into a match for his trousers, and a tartan shirt — he had two of them, one red and one green. Growing on his head were clumps of grizzly blacky-grey hair, all different lengths because he cut it himself.

He seldom talked to anyone, not even when he was in Nagle's supermarket, in the village, getting messages. All he would do was point a dirty finger at what he wanted and grunt. He didn't even talk to Mam when she gave him the scones for his tea. Not that Mam minded; she just said, "God help him, I think the poor man's mind is only half with him, living like he does with only dogs for company. And God help them too, because they seem to be as odd as himself and åabout as friendly." Mam would only laugh when one of the bull terriers — Johnny Mac usually brought them with him in the evenings, when he came to collect the scones — would growl and snap at her.

As he eyed us up and down, I kept on saying that I was sorry, and at the same time I tried to get beside Kevin, to get him to stop laughing and spouting on about how the pong was going to kill all the birds in the area. I knew that if Johnny Mac said anything to Mam about what had happened and about the carry-on of Kevin, she would blame me and I would be grounded for a month. And if Dad got to hear about it, I would probably end up locked in my room like Rapunzel and have to let my hair grow till my prince could rescue me. And the only Prince I knew in the whole of the parish happened to be a dog.

I couldn't get anywhere near Kevin to shut him up. In fact, the nearer I got to him, the worse he became. And, worse still, Johnny Mac's face started to get very red and there was a snarl on his lips more vicious than any of his dogs'.

"Wait'll I get me hands on ye, ye little runt!" Johnny roared, making to cycle after Kevin; but the bag on the carrier wobbled, and he had to put his hand back to steady it. Johnny cursed the bag and then shook his fist at Kevin and shouted, "I'll get ye!"

"Yeah, yeah,
yeah!" Kevin said,
waving his hand at Johnny.
Johnny shook his fist, cursed again and made
another attempt to cycle after Kevin, only to stop
after a few feet to look round and check that the
black bag was still in place. Whatever was in that
bag, he definitely didn't want it ending up on the
ground. Eventually he gave up on the idea of going
after Kevin and eyeballed me and Ruthie out of it
for a few seconds. Then he spat on the ground near

us, turned the bike round and, glancing back every so often at the black bag, cycled slowly away.

God help me when Mam hears about this, I thought, as Kevin the Lunatic ran up beside me.

"Yeah! That was ace," he said, punching the air.

"Well, I'm glad you think so," I said. "You've just got me grounded for life."

"Nah, I haven't."

"Well, what do you think is going to happen when he tells Mam? Who do you think she's going to blame? Not sweet little innocent Kevin."

"Oh yeah — she'll blame you and you'll be grounded," Kevin said, and started hee-hee-ing out of him, which really got to me.

I could have kicked myself for saying anything to him, though I'd rather have kicked him. But what was the point? He was a clown that had escaped from a passing circus. I decided that the best thing to do was to ignore him completely, pretend he didn't exist. I grabbed hold of Ruthie's hand and started to walk.

Five minutes later, Kevin said, "How long more do we have to walk?" I said nothing. He kept on asking me, so I started talking to Ruthie and he got the message and went quiet. He stayed that way until we came to a gate that led into a field.

"Hey, Mary, there's Johnny Mac."

I looked up the field, and there at the top, where the field met the woods, was Johnny.

"What's he doing going into this part of the woods with a black bag?" I said, thinking out loud.

"You think maybe he has something valuable in the bag and is stashing it?" Kevin said, all ears.

"Don't be foolish!" I said. Then I copped that I shouldn't be talking to him, so I just walked on and left him talking to himself. Eventually he got tired doing that and clammed up till we got near the village.

"I know a way that you won't be grounded," he said.

I said nothing.

"I do know a way."

"Oh, sure you do," I said. I didn't mean to open my mouth, but I couldn't help it. "And you also know a secret. You know everything."

"I do know a way."

"No, you don't," I said in a mocking voice, hoping that maybe I could draw the information out of him. The thought of being grounded was beginning to prey on my mind, and I figured that it would be just like the little slimeball to know a way out of this.

"I do, you dork."

"Who do you think you're calling a dork?" I made a grab for him, but he ducked out of the way. "Just you wait!" I shouted at him. "You'll be sorry."

"Not as sorry as you when you're grounded, na-na-na-na na na," he started chanting, running up beside me and then ducking and running away again.

"Ah, shut up, you moron. I don't care."

"You will when all your friends are out playing and you're stuck in your room, na-na-na-na na na. And I know a way that you won't have to be grounded, na-na-na-na na na."

"I don't care, I told you, so button it and go away. You're wrecking my head," I said, but it only made him worse. He kept na-na-na-ing out of him until I finally asked him to tell me the great plan that he had.

"It'll cost you," he said, his face plastered with joy. I looked at him and thought about putting Ruthie sitting up on the wall and running after him and thumping the information out of him, but I knew that if I didn't catch him he would be na-na-ing for the rest of the day and I'd end up going mental.

"How much?"

"You can buy me an ice-cream, a can of orange, a packet of crisps, a big bar of chocolate, a packet of dry roasted nuts, a —"

"No way!"

"Well, if you don't, I won't tell you the plan, na-na-na-na —"

"Forget it, Kevin. I haven't got the money to get you all those things."

Kevin went quiet for a moment. Then he said, "Well, what about if you just buy me three things and come with me someplace?"

"What are you on about, someplace?"

"I'll tell you in a minute, I don't want everyone to hear," he said, pointing down at Ruthie. "Will you come?"

I thought about it. Three things and going someplace didn't feel as bad as buying him a gansey-load of goodies, so I said, "All right, but this plan of yours better be good or else you're dead meat."

"It is."

"Well, tell me."

"I'll tell you after you buy me a can and an ice-cream and a big bar of chocolate and come with me someplace." He gave a little throaty laugh and clapped his hands in expectation. I just looked at him and shook my head.

"Well, at least your mother doesn't have to worry about what you're going to be when you grow up, because you already are what you're going to be," I said, as Ruthie began to moan into my face, again, that she was tired and wanted to be carried.

"What am I going to be?" Kevin said, staring at me with blue eyes that looked like they belonged in the church crib at Christmas.

"Not what you're going to be, I told you — what you already are," I said, bending down so Ruthie could climb up on my back.

"What's that?"

"Don't you know? That doesn't say much for your so-called plan, if you can't figure that one out."

"Tell me," Kevin said, his face full of curiosity.

"A rotten little gangster, that's what."

"Very funny."

"It might be funny, but it's true," I said, as we walked into the village and headed for Nagle's supermarket.

Chapter Five

After we brought Ruthie home – luckily she was too tired to want to come back out with us – I had to go back to the place where we'd seen Johnny Mac go into the woods. Why? Because Kevin, the plank, was sure that Johnny Mac had something really valuable in the black bag. He became even more sure of it when he saw Johnny cycle past the house with no black bag tied to the carrier. I tried to tell Kevin that this was a waste of time, but Know-It-All wouldn't listen.

When we got into the woods, I turned to Kevin and said, "Behind which tree should we start looking, Mr Sherlock Holmes?"

Kevin sighed, looked around at the zillions of trees and sighed again, and kept on sighing. I was about to give him loads of I-told-you-so, but I needed to hear his great plan. Anyway, I was sort of curious myself about what Johnny Mac had in the black bag and why he had brought it to this part of the woods.

Then it hit me. "Come on – I think I know where he might have brought the bag."

"You do?" Kevin said, grinning excitedly. "Where?"

"To a cabin," I said, and walked off without saying another word. I didn't want Kevin moaning into my ear, and he would moan if he knew that we had a twenty-minute walk to get to the cabin. Dad sometimes brought me and Ruthie up there when he felt like going on a safari. Years ago, Dad and the other workers used the cabin for storing stuff and having their tea in, when they were felling trees in this part of the woods.

It took ten minutes – thank God for that, at least – before the first moan of "I don't see no cabin" trickled past Kevin's lips, but it wasn't long before the trickle became a groaning flood. It was just as well that we hadn't too far left to go, because my head was beginning to spin from having to listen to Kevin the Doolally Parrot beside me.

At last we came near to the place where the cabin was, and I was able to turn to Kevin and say, "We're here, so plug it."

"I don't see –"

"Just beyond the covering of ferns up there, where the wood falls away, you'll see a ca–" He was gone before I had finished.

The cabin was down in a kind of a hollow where the wood fell away slightly for a bit. You would never guess that it was there unless you knew about it; it was almost covered by briars and coated with green moss. It was like the wood was trying its best to swallow the cabin.

As I looked down, I could see Kevin over at the door of the cabin, pulling at something. When I got to him, I found that he was trying to loosen a coil of frayed rope that was tightly knotted around an n-shaped piece of iron hammered into the frame of the door. The rope went through a small hole in the door and was attached to something on the inside, and this kept the door closed.

"We should have brought your ma's carving-knife with us," Kevin said, his face getting red with frustration.

"Oh, yeah, Mam would only have been rapt to give it to us, and Johnny Mac would never have guessed that there'd been someone here when he found the rope cut. Some Sherlock Holmes you are." I pushed him aside and pulled at the knot until I got it free.

When I opened the door I was hit by a blast of heat and the smell of a thousand toasted stinky socks and a dog kennel that had never been cleaned. Holding my nose, I stepped inside. In the middle of the floor there was a table with bockety legs. It looked like it was going to topple over from the weight of three things like rabbit-hutches that had been placed on top of it. Under the table was a huge roll of chicken wire.

I didn't get a chance to see what else was in the cabin because the stench had somehow slipped past my fingers and was going down the back of my throat, making me want to puke. I ran outside and left Kevin to have a nose about, which he did for ages, despite the wicked smell. There just had to be a bit of skunk in him.

When he came out he came out with a long face and the smell. "There's no black bag in there," he said, with a groan.

"Well, let's look around out, here," I said, moving away to the left of the cabin. Something that looked like a hole, a little way away, caught my eye. I went to investigate and found that the hole was actually a square pit about four feet deep. At each corner a post about six inches high, and about as thick as my arm, was wedged into the ground.

As I stood there trying to figure out what the pit was for, Kevin came over and moaned at me, "He mustn't've brought the black bag here."

"That's not my fault," I said. "I did my best. Now you just remember that you have to tell me what the plan is, so as I won't get grounded."

"Yeah, I will," he said, sighing into his runners. "Can we go home now? I'm hungry."

*   *   *

Kevin's plan was like himself — simple. At first, when he told me, I felt like I had been taken for a sap. But then, the more I thought about this plan of his, the more I realised that it was the only thing that could be done. If Kevin kept out of the way when Johnny Mac called to the house in the evening, then Johnny Mac wouldn't know that Kevin was staying with us, and he might think that Kevin was one of the neighbours' children and had nothing to do with us at all. He wouldn't know any different; he never really bothered with anyone in the parish, except Mam.

Yes, it might work out all right, if Kevin did stay out of the way. But would he? The more I looked at him as we walked home, the more I began to wonder — wonder if he might change his mind, now that we hadn't found the black bag. And I was right. Oh, he stayed out of the way, just about, but only after I gave him three euro and fifty cents. He wanted five euro, but there was no way I would

45

give it to him: I had to save some bit of pride. Even when I did give him the money, the rat kept going over and looking out the window. My heart was doing cartwheels while I was watching him; I was scared that Johnny Mac would cop his beefy head at the window. And he definitely would have done, except that he hardly stopped to take the scones off Mam.

I really felt like clocking Kevin after his little performance, and I think I would have, only that Dad was sitting at the table having his dinner and he was in a real surly mood. Ruthie was sitting beside him, doing her usual impression of Oliver Twist: asking for more from Dad's plate. She had got into a habit of not eating her dinner unless Dad fed her, and even then it had to be what Dad was eating. Dad used to tease her by putting a spoonful of potatoes close to her lips and making her open her mouth as wide as she could; then he would put the spoon in her mouth and whip it out again before she had time to close her gnashers on the spoon.

That was what used to happen a few aeons ago, when all was bliss on the planet. Now all he did was shovel it into her mouth, the same way as he shovelled coal onto the fire. Sometimes Ruthie would start spluttering out of her as some potato hit the back of her throat; Dad would mumble that he was sorry, but after a while the same thing would happen again, and Mam would have to go over and drag Ruthie away and feed her herself. The same thing happened this evening, except that today Dad had pushed his dinner plate away after only barely touching it. He definitely looked like he was carrying the woes of Job and a half-ton of burning coals on his head.

Still, despite Dad's funeral-face mood, an opportunity arose to get back at Kevin that I couldn't resist. Mam was busy trying to get Ruthie to eat, Dad was sitting just staring out the door, and Kevin was standing at the table, looking out the window after Johnny Mac. I went to the fridge, took out a carton of milk – Dad likes a glass of milk after his dinner – and brought it to the table. On the way, I passed by Kevin and kicked him, by accident, on the ankle. He let such a scream out of him that, had he been on the *Titanic* when it was sinking, the crew on the *Carpathia* would have heard him and everyone would have been rescued.

"What's going on?" Dad said, turning round in his chair.

"I am so sorry, Kevin, I hope I didn't hurt you," I said, in the most innocent voice I could manage. Then, looking at Dad, I quickly added, "I was just getting the milk for you."

"I didn't ask you to get me milk," Dad said, very waspish. "God Almighty, it's hard enough to get you to do what you're supposed –"

"But I got it because I know you always like to have a glass of milk after your dinner," I said, before he had a chance to finish what he was going to say. I know this was sucking up big-time, but it was worth

47

it just to get back at Kevin, just to see the look of anger on his mush.

And, besides, the sucking up that I did was nothing to the sucking up that Kevin did later on that evening. The leech gave Mam the big bar of chocolate I had bought him and whispered something into her ear. The next thing, Mam, the flowerpot, went in while Dad was watching the telly and said, "Joe, Kevin would love to have a ride on one of the donkeys. What do you think?"

"I'll see," Dad said, which is his way of telling you that you can say bye-de-bye to what you want. I was thrilled, but Kevin must have sussed that something was wrong with Dad's answer, because he did some more serious sucking up: he said that he was going up to bed to do some drawing and reading. He gave me a sly grin as he turned to go.

Dad's jaw hit his knees, while Mam's eyes became as wide as dinner plates as they watched Kevin go up the stairs. "Ah, God love him, Joe, but isn't he a grand lad!"

I couldn't believe what I was hearing. How Mam couldn't see through Kevin's little act, I'll never know. And, to really make my night, Dad boomed in with: "It's a pity Mary there wouldn't take a leaf from his book and do something constructive up in her room, instead of listening to that Walkman. No wonder she can't get up in the mornings, and goes around not knowing what she's doing, after lying awake half the night listening to that mindless trash."

Here we go again, I thought. Pick on me, why don't you? Why not blame me for everything that goes wrong? It's all my fault. I felt like shouting at Dad, and I might have done, too, if some stupid tears hadn't come into my eyes. I turned my head so as Dad couldn't see them, and waited a few minutes for the ear-bashing to stop. But he kept going on and on. I endured it for as long as I could, in the hope that he might eventually stop being a pain, but half an hour later he was still giving out. So I just gave up and went upstairs, wondering if there was an age limit on someone ringing Childline.

As I went into my room, I heard Mam saying something to Dad and Dad shouting at her, and then I heard him go out and slam the back door after him. I flung my jeans and T-shirt on the chair and put on my Bart Simpson nightdress that Dad had given me for my surprise at Christmas, and then immediately took it off and threw it in a ball across the room. It went under Ruthie's bed. Tomorrow I would burn it. I went to the wardrobe and took out a nightdress that Mam had bought me, put that on and got into bed. I didn't even say good night to Leonardo; I was too angry and upset with Dad.

It wouldn't have been so bad if Audrey and Laura, my two best friends, had been at home; but with both of them off on the trip, I had no one to talk to. And it would be pointless talking to them when they got back, because they would be full of the great time they'd had. This made me feel even worse. I grabbed my Walkman from the locker beside my bed, put the headphones on, tuned in to Community FM and turned up the volume as loud as it would go.

Later, when I calmed down, I got up out of bed, switched on the light in the hall and went out to the bathroom. When I came back, I looked over at Leonardo and said good night to him. Then I looked again. At first, I thought it was just the shadowy light from the hall playing tricks with Leonardo's face, making him look different; but the more I looked, the more convinced I was that something was wrong with him. Shadowy light or no shadowy light, he wasn't the same Leonardo I had pasted up on the wall.

Now, normally I would never turn on the light in the bedroom, in case Ruthie woke up and started moaning out of her. I have to say here that, though Ruthie is my sister and I love her to bits, I can't wait till she's older and not afraid to sleep on her own. It is a major pain not being able to turn on the light in your own room, I can tell you. Tonight, though, Ruthie could wake up and moan all she liked – the light was going on; this was an emergency.

I turned on the light and stared in horror at Leonardo. Two red horns were growing out of his head, a black moustache was sprouting under his nose, a green goatee was hanging off his chin, and a pipe was sticking out of his mouth. Oh, and three of his teeth had been blacked out to add a sort of hillbilly touch.

Someone in this house was going to die for this, and I knew who. I looked around the room for something heavy to clock Kevin with, but there was nothing except my Simpsons lamp. It had a heavy round base, but it also had a picture of Bart, Homer and Lisa on it, and I couldn't have them coming in contact with a cow-dung-head; they might get contaminated. I felt like screaming: there was nothing in the room that I could hit him with. I tried to think of something suitable from downstairs and immediately thought of several possibilities.

I turned off the light and went slowly and quietly to the top of the stairs; I didn't want to wake either Mam or Dad. But when I got halfway down the stairs, I heard their muffled voices. Mam was saying something about being able to help. I knew that what she was talking about had something to do with Dad's yo-yo moods, but I didn't bother to listen; I was too mad about not being able to go downstairs and get the giant brown toby jug that Mam kept the biscuits in.

Furious, I went back up the stairs and went into the bathroom and brushed my teeth; I nearly brushed the enamel off them, I was in such a temper. I kept thinking of Kevin lying in bed, probably dreaming up another way to get at me, to make my life more miserable than it already was.

I filled the blue plastic tumbler with water and rinsed out my mouth, and I was about to go back to my room when an idea struck me. I refilled the tumbler with cold water, right up to the rim, and then turned off the light in the bathroom — and, most importantly, the one in the hall: I didn't want it to waken the sleeping prince and turn him back into a frog, especially as frogs like water and there was no water in his room. Not yet, anyway.

I walked slowly down the hall, being very careful not to lose a precious drop. When I got to Prince Frog's room, I turned the door handle, as quietly as I could, and very gently pushed the door a crack open. I needn't have worried about waking the Frog; I could hear him croaking his head off.

"Time for your bath, Mr Slurry-Head," I whispered, as I pushed the door open a fraction more so as I could squeeze into the room. That fraction was one fraction too much. A crashing sound exploded in the room. Kevin had put a chair up against the door.

My hand shook with the fright, and half the water went down the front of my nightdress. Kevin jumped out of bed, and before I had time to fling the rest of the water at him, Mam came up the stairs and turned the light on in the hall. I moved quickly away from Kevin's door.

"What in heaven's name is going on up here?" Mam hissed.

I was very tempted to tell her what Kevin had done, but I wasn't going to have him going around calling me a tell-tale for the rest of the weekend; no way was I going to give him that satisfaction.

"I was just getting a drink of water, and I tripped and fell," I said, my face reddening.

"Well, if you'd turned on the light you wouldn't have fallen," Mam said, looking at me suspiciously. "And you shouldn't be drinking water out of the tap in the bathroom."

"I didn't want the light to wake Kevin and Ruthie," I said, but the look on Mam's face told me that she wasn't swallowing it. "And I was afraid to go downstairs in case Dad started giving out to me again," I added quickly. I didn't feel too bad about saying that, because it was partly true.

"Well, your Dad has a lot on his mind — and you tripping around in the dark doesn't help, I can tell you. Now go and change that nightdress."

Well, how was I supposed to know what Dad had on his mind, when no one would tell me? And he wasn't the only one with a lot on his mind. I felt like saying that to Mam, but what was the point? I just put the tumbler back in the bathroom, as she went downstairs.

Then, as I was going into my room to change my nightdress, I heard a sniggering sound. I looked over at Kevin's door. It was a crack open and I could just see his nose. He reminded me of a mouse looking out of a hole, except he was no mouse; he was a cross between a rat and a fox. I sneered at him and went into my room. He would pay for this — he would *die* for this.

Chapter Six

The next morning, with my ears ringing from Mam roaring at me to get up, I inspected the damage done to Leonardo. He looked even worse with the sun shining through the window: he looked like someone who belonged in a freak show. I felt like crying, but I didn't. There would definitely be no tears. Not yet. Not till Kevin was under six feet of clay — and a ton of concrete, if I could manage it, but definitely a few big boulders just to make sure that he stayed down. Then I would bawl and scream and rock my head like you see those men on the telly doing in front of the Wailing Wall.

I would have to make it look good or else some- one might cop on, but I knew that I would find it very, very difficult not to laugh my head off when Kevin was being buried. I would have to peel an onion before I went to his funeral — that always makes you cry — and if anyone got suspicious about the smell of onions, I could always say that I was after eating cheese-and-onion crisps. I would keep a packet in my pocket, for proof. I also decided that I would have to peel onions for a few days after the funeral, as well, just to be on the safe side. I mean, it wouldn't do if I were seen dancing around the place like one of the ballerinas in *Swan Lake*, though I would have to fight hard to resist the temptation.

Then I started thinking about what would happen if I did get caught. I'd probably be sent to one of those prisons like the one on that television programme. I'd be forced to eat cold watery porridge for breakfast, for the rest of my life, and I'd end up being picked on by the other prisoners because I'd be the youngest one there. Just thinking about it made my heart race with fright.

But then I started thinking that maybe Leonardo might come to see me when he read that I had killed because of what was done to his poster. I could see Leonardo trying to break me out of prison, but getting caught, and then the two of us trying to break out together. I could see us pushing crazily at the bars and the guards telling us to get back, the way they were telling himself and Kate Winslet to do on the *Titanic*. I was enjoying these thoughts when Mam roared up and asked me if I was getting up before it got dark. I don't know what her problem was; it wasn't even twelve o'clock yet.

"I am doing this for you," I said, looking at the defaced poster of Leonardo. I put on my jeans, runners and a clean white T-shirt, brushed my teeth and went downstairs to join the ogre for breakfast — his last.

As I sat there, eating a slice of toast and looking at his puss leering across the table at me, I decided how the gruesome deed would be carried out. I knew this way would mean that I would be caught, but after what he had done to the poster of Leonardo, there really wasn't any other way. I would wear the gloves I wore to school in winter; I wasn't going to make it too easy for the gardaí to suss that it was me. But, gloves or no gloves, Kevin had to be throttled for what he had done.

The only problem now was how I was going to get him on his lonesome. Mam, I knew, would want me to go to the shops for her, but Ruthie would more than likely want to come as well. And I would never catch hold of him while Ruthie was with me.

As it was, you would swear that he knew what I was planning to do. He kept on watching me, and as soon as I got up to put a slice of bread in the toaster, he moved his chair away from the table so he could make a run for it if I went to grab him. I have to say that I was tempted, especially as Mam had gone upstairs; but what was the point? If I did manage to catch the little eel, he would only scream his head off. And, besides, it would take ages to throttle that hard neck of his, and I wanted to take my time and do it slowly — make him suffer.

The problem of getting Kevin on his own was solved when Mam came down from upstairs and said, "Mary, will you get the shopping trolley and go down to Nagle's for me? I've made a list of what I want."

I nearly went spare when she mentioned bringing a shopping trolley. I could just imagine the slagging I was going to get when that banana Patrick Caffrey and his friend Dermot "Three Brain Cells" Reid saw me. Every Saturday, they spend the whole day hanging around outside Nagle's supermarket, chewing gum and slagging everybody that passes by, and every Saturday I hear the same twaddle — "Aren't you a great little girlie altogether, to be doing the shopping for your Mammy?" — which I just ignore. Still, I didn't want it on my conscience that I had stretched Dermot's brain cells past their limit by tempting him to come up with a new remark when he saw me with the shopping trolley.

I was going to tell Mam that there was no way that I was bringing it with me, but then she said, "Kevin can go with you; Ruth can stay here with me." How could I refuse? Dermot would just have to risk damaging those three brain cells of his; this opportunity could not be missed.

As we were going out the door, Mam handed Kevin two euro and said, "You're not to be spending your money on me, though I have to say it was most thoughtful and considerate of you." She paused to treat me to one of her withering looks. "I hope others have learned from your kind example." I grabbed the trolley and left before I had to go searching for a sick-bag.

The farther away I got from the house, the better I felt. At least now I didn't have to listen to Mam's song of praise to Kevin, though I had to listen to Kevin calling me "Mrs Doubtfire". I pretended that I couldn't hear him above the rattling noise that the shopping trolley was making as I dragged it along the road.

Eventually Kevin got tired of shouting and walked along quietly behind me — but not too far behind, I was pleased to see. I glanced back a few times, to see what the chances were like of me catching him if I dropped the trolley and ran at him. He was definitely getting closer; maybe the heat from the sun was getting to him, making him drowsy. But he wasn't really close enough for me to feel certain that I'd catch him. I would have to wait for him to get nearer.

I started to walk a little slower, and he didn't notice. In fact, from the look on his dish, I figured he was making up the list of goodies that he was going to demand for keeping out of Johnny Mac's way this evening. I couldn't help smiling as I thought about how permanently Kevin was going to be keeping out of the way.

"Hey, Mary, what ya smiling about?" Kevin said, getting very close to being within range of my grasp.

"That's for me to know and you to find out," I said, praying that he would come just a little bit closer. But he didn't. In fact, he stopped. I kept walking, just to make it look good.

"I know why you're smiling," he called after me.

I stopped and turned round to look at him. "That doesn't surprise me. Sure, you know everything," I laughed. Then I walked slowly on. For a moment I thought I had blown it; there wasn't a peep out of him, and I couldn't see him at all when I took a sly look behind. But then he came running after me, shouting, "I know why you're smiling; you're smiling 'cause you're a spacer!"

I knew that the right thing to do was to ignore him and keep walking; but, whether he was within range or not, I couldn't let him get away with calling me a spacer. I let the shopping trolley fall to the ground and ran after him.

It was like going after Road Runner, he was so fast on his feet. I knew then that Kevin's father had to have been a greyhound. I ran after him till I thought my heart would burst, but, no matter how hard I tried, I couldn't get near him. Then he started getting cocky – running towards me and then, when I went to grab him, turning around and racing off in the opposite direction. It was one of these times when he was turning round to run that he tripped over himself and

fell into the ditch. I was on top of him before he had time to say "Nee-neep."

I wrapped my hands around his throat, but I hadn't got the energy to squeeze a pimple, never mind his neck. So I just sat on him and waited for my breath, along with my energy, to come back.

"Let me up. Let me up," he pleaded for ages. Finally, his face getting red from my weight on top of him, he said, "I'll tell you what your da was telling your ma the other night, if you do."

I had forgotten about that, but now that I had the chance of finding out what the secret was, I decided I might as well hear it, especially as these were going to be Kevin's last words. "Tell me first and then I'll let you up," I lied.

"You let me up first."

"No! You tell me." I pressed my weight on him until he began to resemble Mister Bashful from the Mister books that Ruthie had.

"Okay, I'll tell you!"

I eased my weight off him, just enough that he could speak.

"Your da has something. . . ." He stopped and started aagh-ing out of him and moaning that he couldn't breathe. I stood up, dragging him with me. I made sure to keep a good hold of the neck of his T-shirt, in case he tried to do a runner.

"My dad has what?" I said, moving my left hand onto Kevin's throat. His shifty little eyes were dancing about in his head.

"Has something serious wrong with his heart. He'll have to give up working in the forestry."

61

"What?" I said, the shock making me loosen my grip on Kevin. In a second, he was gone. Not that I cared; Dad having something wrong with his heart and having to give up work was more important than Kevin.

No wonder Dad was always in a mood. I thought about what would happen if he couldn't work any more. How would he pay the mortgage?

Kevin the Lunatic was running around shouting, making everything ten times worse. "You're all going to end up living in a caravan like gypsies!" he said, laughing as loud as he could.

"No we won't," I said; but, as I watched him run off and disappear around a bend in the road, I knew he was right. How could we afford to live in a house if Dad wasn't working?

I could just imagine the slagging that I was going to have to endure when those two peanuts Dermot Reid and Patrick Caffrey saw me, Mam, Dad, and Ruthie living in a caravan. And what would the girls at school say? But it was going to be either a caravan or else going to live with Kevin and his mam. And there was no way that I could possibly listen to Motor-Mouth three hundred and sixty-five days of the year. I would end up going completely gaga — although I probably would anyway, from having to go around all the time with a hood over my head and one of those yashmaky things over my face. And I would definitely be doing that: there was no way I was going to have people gawking at me and saying, "There's that girl that used to live in a house and now lives in a caravan, God love her." I would have to get Ruthie to cover up, as well, but that wouldn't be too much of a problem; she liked wearing Mam's clothes when Mam wasn't watching, especially her high-heeled shoes.

Of course, I might be able to stay with Audrey or Laura; either one of their families might keep me. That way I wouldn't have to live in a caravan at all. This brought hope to my heart; but then I started thinking about Mam and Dad and Ruthie alone in the caravan, and I began to think that it wouldn't be right to abandon them like that. It would be sort of like the *Home Alone* film, except this would be *Home Alone in a Caravan*. I felt bad about that; but then I thought that if I were to spend, say, three days with Laura's family and two days with Audrey's family and the weekends with my family in the caravan, then that wouldn't be too bad. Would it?

I was warming to this idea when a car came speeding around the bend. The driver blasted the horn and shouted out the window at me to get the heck (or something like that) in off the road. With so many thoughts going round in my head, I had wandered into the middle of the road.

I jumped back onto the roadside and watched the car till it was out of sight. I was trying to see if I knew the driver, or the man sitting beside him. I didn't think I did, but the way things were going, it would just be my luck if the man driving the car knew my mam and dad really well — not only that, but called in to see them this evening and told them about me walking in the middle of the road. Dad would definitely lose the head if he heard that, and maybe have a huge heart attack, and then I would really be in it.

As I walked along the road, I began to feel really guilty about all the bad things that I had wished on Dad. And then I got annoyed. I mean, how was I to know that there was something wrong with Dad's heart when neither Mam nor Dad would tell me? I would want

to be one of those — what do they call them? sidekicks, something like that — to know what was going on. Anyway, things wouldn't have been half as bad at all if Kevin hadn't come down for the weekend. I should have choked him when I had the chance — and now that I could hear him hollering "Yahoo" and laughing his hyena head off, I wished I had.

I walked on, thinking that Kevin had to be laughing at himself, because he sounded hysterical; but then I thought about Mam's trolley, and I started to run. I had a very bad feeling about what I was going to see when I got around the bend. And my feeling was right.

I could have cried. Kevin was standing there, laughing his heart out, with tears streaming down his cheeks. His right hand was holding the shopping trolley, which was now in the shape of a V.

"What did you do to the trolley?" I shouted, running towards him.

"I didn't do nothing," he said, going all serious. "It was run over by a car. You should have seen it, Mary. The driver went out of his way to go over it."

"Why didn't you move it in off the road?"

"Why did you leave it in the middle of the road? You dork." He started laughing again.

"This is not funny, Kevin. Mam is going to throw a right wobbler when she sees this."

"Yahoo!" he said.

"Ah, shut up!" I roared at him, as I picked up the trolley and tried to straighten it. I didn't want to apply too much force, as I was afraid that it would snap completely and I would have no trolley to bring home the messages in. I finally managed to get it fairly straight, though there was still a bit of a dinge in it. I wheeled it along the road after me to see how it went. One of the wheels was all right, but the other one was slightly up in the air. This was just great. God only knew what Mam was going to say when she saw it — never mind what Dad would say. I felt like screaming. What else was going to go wrong on me? Why did everything have to happen this year, just in the last few months? Why couldn't things have stayed like they were last year, with no hassles?

Last year we had all gone on picnics, and Dad had brought me up to Dublin a few times; now the only place we went together was to Mass. Last year we had had a house to live in and Dad had been healthy; now it looked like we were all going to be living in a caravan and maybe have to take up knitting Aran sweaters or selling the *Big Issue* to make money — and no one around here ever bought the *Big Issue*, or, for that matter, wore Aran sweaters. It was all so unfair.

As I walked along the road, I felt my head drop onto my chest and tears come into my eyes. I turned my head towards the ditch, so as Kevin wouldn't spot the tears, but of course he did; he would spot a white rabbit lying in a field of snow, even if the rabbit was wrapped in a white blanket.

"What're you crying like a baby for?" he said, sniggering.

"I am not crying like a baby," I said, in a jittery voice. "Now go away and leave me alone, Kevin. I'm not in the humour for you." I started to walk quicker.

"Ah, you girls are always crying about something," he said, and started boo-hoo-ing out of him.

"I'll give you something to cry about if I catch you," I told him, getting angry again.

"Ah, you couldn't catch your breath," he said, and snorted. I ignored him and walked on. There was no winning with him; I really don't know why I even bothered.

When I came out of Nagle's supermarket, I had to endure more torment, this time from Patrick Caffrey and Dermot Reid. "Why don't you bring that trolley to the hospital and get its limp fixed?" they kept asking, between sniggers. They didn't bother me, to tell the truth, because I was so relieved that the trolley was still in one piece – though I made sure to put only the bread, cereal, toilet-rolls, biscuits, washing powder, cans of beans, and cans of peas in the trolley. The chicken, bacon, milk and two-litre bottles of lemonade, and the can of orange for myself, I put into plastic bags that I carried by hand, just in case the trolley collapsed with the weight.

A little way down the road, Kevin offered to carry one of the bags. I doubted if I could trust him, but I had no choice, unless I wanted to arrive home with my left arm the same length as a gorilla's: the bags weighed a ton.

"I swear I won't mess," he said. "I'll carry one of the bags for you, if you give me your can of orange."

"You always want something. Do you ever just do something for someone out of the goodness of your heart?"

"No!" he said, tearing the wrapper off the ice-cream that he had bought. He threw the wrapper on the ground.

"Waste of space," I mumbled, as I handed him the can of orange. I gave him the bag with the chicken and meat in it, just in case he got smart and tried to eat what was in it; I held on to the one with the lemonade and milk.

As we went up the road, I had to suffer the sight of Kevin eating the ice-cream, his pinky-red tongue, which was as big as a bath towel, slobbering all over it. The only good thing was that eating it kept him quiet, except for the odd time that he took it into his head to make a "mmm" sound and say, "This is really delicious — scrumptious! Mmmm, just the thing for a hot day!" which sounded like something he had heard in an advert on the telly.

But, advert or not, it was really warm. The sun was making tar blisters the size of melons on the road, and ice-cream followed by a can of orange would be just the thing to cool a body down. . . . Now he had me at it. It had to be the heat.

Chapter Seven

Kevin kept quiet for most of the way home; he was busy stuffing his face with crisps and chocolate, like a proper little pig, and making burping sounds just to annoy me. The only time he spoke was when we passed a red car that was parked in front of a gate that led into a field.

"Hey, Mary, that's the car that nearly creased your ma's trolley," he said, running over and dodging around the car. I kept on walking, and he started calling after me: "Mary! Mary! C'm'ere, you have to see this." He waved his hand at me. I wasn't going to bother, but the way he was crouching and peeping into the field made me curious.

As I went over, Kevin started flapping his hand wildly, like a bird flapping its wing trying to take off. "Get down or they'll see you!"

Stooping, I went to have a look at what was getting Kevin so excited. Probably nothing, I thought; and I was right. Halfway up the field, two men stood talking to Johnny Mac. One of the men was over six feet tall and as skinny as an eyelash, and wore a grey suit; the other one was about a foot shorter and shaped like a beer barrel, and he was wearing a brown jacket and black trousers.

Johnny had his bike with him, and there was a shovel tied to the crossbar.

"I don't know what you're getting so worked up about," I said. "Don't tell me you never saw three people talking before." I went to straighten up, but I was grabbed by a hand and pulled back down.

"But did you not see that Johnny Mac has a black bag with him again?" Kevin said, getting all contrary.

"So? Maybe he brings his lunch around in a black bag," I said. The thought of throttling Kevin, now that I had another chance, came invitingly to mind. But what would be the point? Mam and Dad would probably erect a statue to him in the front garden.

"Well, how come they were all looking into the bag a few seconds ago?" He looked up the field. "See, they're at it again."

I moved past him and peeked through the bars of the gate. He was right: they were all staring into the bag, and then one of the men, the tall thin one, started looking anxiously around.

"What do you think they're up to?" Kevin said, leaning past me to have another peep.

"I don't know and I don't care. Now come on; it's time we got out of here, before those two men see us and think we're messing with their car." I moved back.

"Ah, wait," Kevin pleaded. "Just let's watch them for another few minutes."

"No. You can watch them if you want; I'm in enough trouble as it is. Now come on."

"If you wait, I'll tell you the plan I have so that you won't get into trouble with your ma over the state of the shopping trolley," he said, glancing at me before looking up the field again.

"All your plans cost money and I don't have any more money, and I don't trust you, not after what you did to my Leonardo poster," I said, feeling my temper rise as I thought about poor Leonardo.

"This won't cost you any-thing."

"If you don't want money then what do you want?" I said, tempted by the thought of not having to put up with an ear-bashing from Mam over the trolley. Not that I thought I could trust Kevin the Gunge or anything, but if his plan wasn't going to cost me money, then I didn't see how I could lose. Unless he wanted my Walkman, and there was no way he was getting that, no matter how good his plan was.

Of course, I could have bashed the plan out of him, now that he was crouched in front of me; but I knew he would scream his head off and the two men and Johnny Mac would come running down the field and Johnny would cop Kevin, and then I would be in trouble, big-time. I could just imagine Mam's and Dad's faces if Johnny Mac went and told them about Kevin, about me walking in the middle of the road, about me leaving the shopping trolley in the middle of the road, and then about me trying to kill Kevin. Dad would definitely have me put into the cracker factory after hearing all that.

"C'm'ere and I'll tell you. And keep your voice down," Kevin said, beckoning me over. Telling myself that I was a fool, I moved up beside him.

"What's your plan, Brains?"

"I'll tell your ma that I tripped and fell on the trolley."

"Mam won't believe that."

"Yes she will."

"No she won't, and anyway, you'll probably change your mind at the last minute and not tell her at all."

"I will tell her, if you'll come back here with me. And this time we follow Johnny Mac and see where he hides the bag."

"I am not coming back here to follow Johnny Mac over a stupid bag with nothing in it," I said, moving away again.

"There's something in it," Kevin said, coming after me.

"Of course there is. It's full of money, or maybe diamonds," I said, laughing. "And Johnny Mac is Long John Silver and you're Indiana Jones." I headed back to the trolley.

Kevin ran after me and grabbed my arm. "Mary! Mary, I think I know what Johnny Mac has in the bag," he said, his eyes popping out of their sockets.

"What has he got in the bag, then, oh wise one?" I pulled my wrist away from him.

Kevin looked behind him and then climbed up on the wall to have another gander into the field before coming back over to me. "I'd say the bag is full of drugs, and he's going to hide them up in the woods someplace."

"You're a header," I said. "And I'm not coming back anywhere near here, no matter what you say to Mam."

"I'll give you the money to buy a new poster, as well, if you do."

"No you won't."

"I will. I swear."

"Show me the money, then; the poster costs seven euro," I said, the thought of getting a new Leonardo poster making my heart race.

"I haven't got seven euro, but I'll get it off my ma when she comes to collect me."

"You will, all right," I said, turning away.

"I will! I'll get ten off her for you, if you like."

"I don't believe you." I grabbed the trolley and the bag and left him looking into the field.

The next thing I knew, he was buzzing around me like a bluebottle trying to get out a window. "I will, I will. I swear it!" he said, all in a panic. "Cross my heart." He stuck out his bath towel of a tongue, licked his finger and quickly made a big X across his chest.

"That doesn't mean anything. When your mother comes, you won't ask her for the money, and if you do, you won't give it to me," I said.

"I will. I swear. I swear," Kevin said, nodding his head.

"Well, then, swear on your dad's grave."

"Okay."

"No, say you swear." There was no way I was letting him off that easy.

"I swear."

"On your dad's grave."

"I swear on my da's grave that I will give you seven euro," he said, staring down at the ground with a sad look on his face.

"Ten euro," I said, and he nodded. "All right. Let's go home — and just you remember that you swore on your dad's grave."

We hurried along the road. I felt a bit bad about making Kevin swear on his dad's grave, but how else could I trust him to give me the money? And, anyway, it was his own fault: I wouldn't have made him swear at all, only he did what he did to Leonardo. I just hoped Mam would never find out about it. She would go mental if she did. She says that you should never swear — that it is a sin, a mortal sin.

Chapter Eight

When we got home, Kevin kept the first part of his promise: he told Mam that he had tripped and fallen on the trolley.

"Are you all right? Are you sure you haven't hurt yourself?" Mam said, all concerned. She never mentioned a word about the trolley, but if it had been me that came in and said I had fallen on it, there is no way she would have been so sympathetic. No, she would have gone loop-the-loop and lashed me out of it.

Getting back out proved to be tricky.

"Can I come with you?" Ruthie said, grabbing my hand.

"I can't bring you with me now," I said, freeing my hand. "I'm in a big hurry."

"What big hurry are you in?" Mam said, stopping taking the messages out of the trolley.

"I – ah. . . ." I didn't know what to say, but Slick-Tongue Kevin did.

"Mary's going to help me look for the money I lost."

"Oh, did you lose money?" Mam said, tch-tching out of her. "How much did you lose?"

"Five euro," Kevin said. The dirty little liar didn't even blink.

"Well, don't worry if you can't find it; I'll give you the money you lost."

"You're the very best, Auntie Helen!" He ran over and gave her a hug.

"Thank you, Kevin. That's very nice of you," Mam said, thrilled to the teeth with herself.

I ran out the door before I got sick. I just couldn't believe that Mam was swallowing the bosh Kevin was giving her. If Mam had been on the *Titanic*, it would never have sunk: she could have swallowed the iceberg whole, and half the sea as well.

We ran up the road, or rather Kevin ran; I just jogged after him, listening to him moaning at me to hurry up. I ignored his moans. Anyway, he hadn't gone very far when he turned around and ran back.

"Mary! Mary! They're coming!" he shouted, his eyes dancing about in his head. As he stood beside me, panting, I saw the red car speeding in our direction.

"Just act natural and walk," I said, because there was nothing else to do. The car whizzed by us without even slowing down and without either of the two sour-faced men in the front even bothering to look at us.

"Did you see the state of their faces?" Kevin said, getting even more excited. "They're dealers!"

"How would you know?"

"Johnny Mac must be hiding the drugs for them," Kevin said, ignoring my question. "Hey, Mary, we're going to be rich!" He started dancing around the road like Tinkerbell. "All we have to do is find that

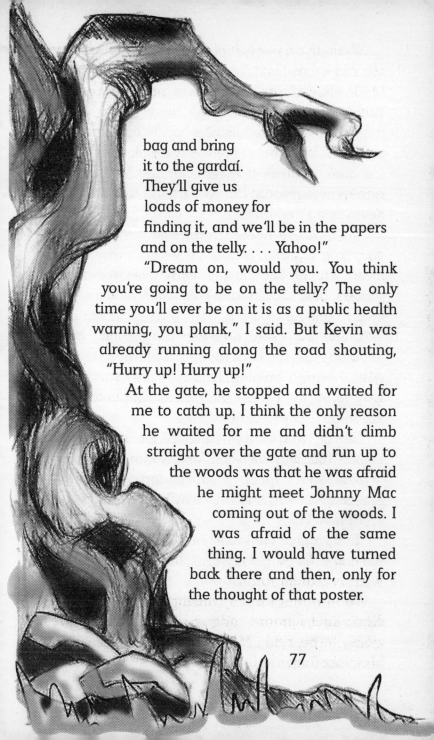

bag and bring
it to the gardaí.
They'll give us
loads of money for
finding it, and we'll be in the papers
and on the telly. . . . Yahoo!"

"Dream on, would you. You think you're going to be on the telly? The only time you'll ever be on it is as a public health warning, you plank," I said. But Kevin was already running along the road shouting, "Hurry up! Hurry up!"

At the gate, he stopped and waited for me to catch up. I think the only reason he waited for me and didn't climb straight over the gate and run up to the woods was that he was afraid he might meet Johnny Mac coming out of the woods. I was afraid of the same thing. I would have turned back there and then, only for the thought of that poster.

We hadn't gone far into the woods when Kevin spotted a bike chained to a fir tree. It was Johnny Mac's bike, all right; there was no mistaking that. The saddle was in bits, the black frame was all chipped and the pedals had hardly any rubber left on them. I started to feel a bit spooky when I saw the bike, because it meant Johnny Mac could be somewhere nearby. I moved away from it and told Kevin to do the same.

"Yeah, you're right," Kevin said, his voice dropping to a whisper. "He could be watching us right now." He looked at me with eyes the size of saucers, blue saucers, and I felt something like an icy finger skate up my back.

"Come on," I said, half-expecting Johnny Mac to jump up from the thick covering of ferns over on the right. I started walking; I didn't really know where I was going, but I knew that it was a lot better for us not to be caught near that bike.

"Maybe we should spread out," Kevin said, after a while. "That way we'll find Johnny Mac a lot quicker."

"And what happens if you get lost? You haven't a breeze of how to find your way back," I said.

"Course I do."

"Yeah, right. Well, you can scrap the spreading-out idea. We'll go towards the cabin; maybe he went in that direction."

We must have been walking for fifteen minutes when Kevin started nudging me in the ribs with his elbow. "There he is!" he said, jabbing the air with his index finger.

"Where?" I said, my heart beginning to beat faster at the thought that Johnny Mac might be very near us. He wasn't. I spotted him walking between the trees, a shovel over his shoulder, way over to the right of us. My heart beat easier.

"Hey, Mary, he hasn't got the black bag with him!" Hawkeye Kevin said, jumping about all over the place. "He must've left it at the cabin."

"Will you stay easy and get down, or he'll see you!" I dragged Kevin down behind a tree.

"No, he won't," Kevin whined. "I want to go."

"Just give him a few minutes, to make sure he's well gone, and then we'll go."

A second later, Kevin popped up his head, looked around, and said, "But he's gone now."

"But there's nothing stopping him from coming back, so we wait a few minutes just to be sure," I said, grabbing his arm.

"How many minutes?" Kevin said, trying to pull away from me.

"A few," I said, tightening my grip on his arm. "You're worse than Ruthie. Can you not stay easy?"

"Not with you holding my arm," Kevin said, sneering.

"Don't start, or I'll go home and leave you here."

Kevin snorted, but he stayed quiet — for about a minute.

"Can we go now, Mary? Plee-ease," he said, scrunching up his face.

I looked round. I figured if Johnny Mac had been going to come back, he would have done it by now.

"All right," I said, letting go of Kevin's arm. "But don't make any noise."

I might as well have told Sap-Brain to bang a drum and jump up in the air, because he started yahooing out of him as he charged away, like a bull being chased by a bumblebee with a bad attitude, in the direction of the cabin. If Johnny Mac had been anywhere close by he would have heard Kevin; in fact, the people in the next parish must have heard him, even if they had their ears plugged. I went after him, furious with myself for having got involved in this nonsense. I should have choked him and forgotten about the ten euro, poster or no poster.

When I got to the cabin, Kevin was coming out. "It's not there," he said, and from the look on his face I thought he was going to cry.

"Well, look around the outside. He had to be coming from here," I said, as I went over to investigate the square pit.

A few minutes later, Kevin dashed over to me, barely able to speak with excitement.

"Mary, Mary, I found the black bag in the bushes, and it's real heavy!" he said in a screechy voice. He pulled me by the arm over to the side of the cabin. Just beside a tangle of bushes was a bulky black bag, tied at the neck with elastic bands.

Kevin dived on the bag and, his eyes glinting with greed, reefed the elastics off and pulled open the mouth of the bag. Next moment, he jumped up. "This is a stupid place with stupid people!" he said, and gave the bag an unmerciful kick. Then he turned his back to me and went into a sulk.

While he was sulking, I put the elastics back around the neck of the bag and pushed it back into the bushes. He was right, the bag was real heavy; but then, the dozens of cans inside it weren't filled with feathers. I tried to figure out why Johnny Mac would leave loads of cans of beer up here, but I couldn't figure anything out, because Kevin started ranting out of him about how brainless we all were, and his voice was going straight through my head.

I stood up. I was about to say that we were going home when I thought of something.

"Kevin, shut up, will you, and help me find a spot that's been dug up."

"What?"

"A place that's freshly dug. Johnny Mac brought a shovel up here with him, and he wasn't bringing it for a walk. He must have been burying something."

"Another black bag — the one with the drugs in it!" Kevin said, and went running all over the place with his head bowed so low that he looked like he was sniffing the ground.

Less than five minutes later, he shouted at me that he had found the spot; and he had. We both got down on our knees and used our fingers to scoop out the earth.

"Don't scatter the earth all over the place, we'll need it to refill the hole," I said, as Kevin pawed at the ground like a hungry dog looking for a favourite bone. He slowed up for a minute, but the excitement got to him again and he tore at the ground like a JCB gone mad. There was earth going everywhere — up in the air, onto his T-shirt, and onto his face, where it stuck to the sweat under his nose and traced a bit of a moustache. And then suddenly he stopped and looked at me, with his mouth open so wide that I could see the filling in one of his back teeth.

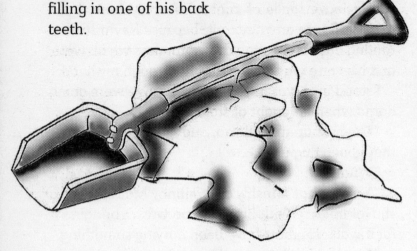

"I've found it," he said.

I have to say that I found myself getting a bit excited as well. Not that I thought there was going to be anything in the bag except junk of some kind — but still.

We both scraped the earth away from around the bag. Then, just as I was about to lift it up, Kevin snatched it away from me. "Lemme open it," he said, and put the bag on the ground beside him. Then he twisted sideways, so I couldn't see, and plunged his hand into the bag.

Next thing he let a roar out of him and shot his hand up in the air, like he was in class and the teacher had said, "Hands up anyone who knows the answer to this." I looked at Kevin's hand and let out a roar myself. His hand was smeared with blood.

"What happened?" I said, thinking that there must have been broken glass in the bag. But then, as Kevin leaned back and wiped his hand on the ground, I saw what was in the bag, and I started to feel sick. Then I started to feel angry and disgusted with Johnny Mac.

I looked at Kevin. He was staring down at the bag, his face as white as milk.

"Why did he do that?" Kevin said, after a while.

"I don't know. I don't know," I said, feeling my eyes fill.

"Did he do it with the shovel?"

"What are you asking me that for?"

"He shouldn't have done it."

"I know," I said. Tears were taking the place of my anger. "Come on, put the bag back into the ground and I'll cover it up, and we can go home."

"Not before I see how many there are." Kevin bent down and ripped the bag wide open. I looked down, and when I saw that there were five of them, I couldn't bear it, so I turned my head away and cried.

"Hey, Mary, one of them is moving!"

"What?" I said, blinking the tears out of my eyes.

"Yeah, I think one of them is still alive. Look, he's breathing." Kevin lifted up a tiny white puppy, with a face that was streaked with blood, from the group of five.

"Oh God! Let me hold him."

"He's blessed that he's so small; that's how he must've missed being bashed by the shovel," Kevin said as he handed me the pup.

It fitted snugly into my left hand, and as I held it, its little body started trembling. I stroked it gently with my right hand, and its little eyelids opened and I could see the grey-blue colour of its eyes. I started to cry again.

"What yeh crying for when he's alive?" Kevin said.

"Shut up, Kevin," I said, between sobs. I turned the pup over in my hand, just to make sure it wasn't hurt underneath, and discovered something else. "And he's not a he, he's a she," I said, gaining some control over my tears.

"What yeh going to do with him – I mean her?"

"I'm going to keep her."

"And what are you going to tell your ma and da?"

"I'm not going to tell them anything yet. I'm just going to keep her out in the back shed till I can think of something." I didn't fancy telling either Mam or Dad how I had got the pup. The way Dad's mood was, you wouldn't know how he might react. I would tell Mam, but I would have to wait for the right moment.

"You're going to get caught," Kevin said.

"I won't if you keep your mouth shut – and you better, Kevin. This is serious."

"I'm not a squealer."

"Yeah, right. Don't tell me you wouldn't have gone and shown your face to Johnny Mac yesterday evening, only I gave you money."

"Might have done, but I wouldn't have squealed."

"That would have been a big help."

"But I didn't go out, did I?"

"Ah, shut up, Kevin, and put that bag and the pups back into the ground so as we can go home."

Kevin put the bag and the four pups into the hole, and I gently covered them over with earth.

Chapter Nine

I went home a different way – a longer way, but it brought us out at the part of the woods behind our house. Kevin walked beside me the whole time, without so much as one moan out of him. Maybe he was thinking about the terrible thing that Johnny Mac had done. I know I was.

When we passed Jaws and Slug, Kevin regained his voice. "I sure would love to ride around on one of them," he said, gazing longingly at the donkeys.

"Never mind the donkeys; this is more important. I need to figure out a way to get the box from my runners out of my wardrobe and into the shed, without anyone seeing me."

"I could help you get it, if you give me three euro."

"What did you say? You're not getting a –"

"Ah, take a chill pill, would yeh? I'm only joking. I'll help," Kevin said, a big smirk returning to his face.

"This is no time to be joking. And you better help me get milk out for the pup, as well."

Kevin nodded, and mumbled something like "Yes, Mammy," under his breath.

"Now, all you have to do is make sure Mam isn't looking my way when I come downstairs with the box. But first we better have a bit of a wash in the rain barrel at the back of the house. Mam's bound to get suspicious if she sees the state of our hands."

"What about if Ruthie sees you taking the box?"

"Oh, no!" I had never thought about Ruthie. If she saw me with a box she would follow me, and I knew she would never be able to keep quiet about the pup. "This is a disaster," I said. And then, as I looked up at the bathroom window, I thought of another way to get the box.

After we washed our hands, I went into the house and told Mam, when she asked where Kevin was, that he would be in in a minute. Dad was sitting at the far end of the table, drawing on a sheet of paper; Ruthie was on a chair beside him, her tongue sticking out of the corner of her mouth as she followed every move of his pencil. She didn't even look up at me as I went upstairs.

I got the box out of my wardrobe, folded an old T-shirt into it and went into the bathroom. I opened the window – but first I flushed the toilet, so Mam and Dad wouldn't hear – and threw the box down to Kevin. I waited till I heard him coming in before I went back downstairs.

"Did you find the money that you lost?" I heard Mam say to Kevin as I went over to the fridge.

"No, and me and Mary looked everywhere," he said, with such innocence that I was sure a halo was going to appear around his head. "Didn't we, Mary?" He turned and looked at me.

What could I say? In fact, I said nothing. I just nodded and opened the fridge door, before the flush of red that I could feel on my neck spread up into my face. I took out a carton of milk and poured some into a glass.

"How much did you lose, son?" I heard Dad ask.

"Well, I thought it was five euro I'd lost, Uncle Joseph, but it was seven: three two-euro coins and a one-euro."

I nearly choked on my first sip of milk when I heard that. Compared to Kevin, Pinocchio was definitely a saint.

"Well, here's the seven euro for you," Dad said, reaching into his pocket.

"Ah no, it's all right, Uncle Joseph. I couldn't take it."

"Why not?"

Kevin looked down at the floor and, I swear to God, started to blush. "Me mammy wouldn't like me to." What an actor. He deserved ten Oscars for this performance.

"Don't mind your mammy," Dad said, pretending to be annoyed. "Take that seven euro, do you hear me?"

"Yes. Do," Mam urged.

While this drippy drivel was going on, I grabbed a slice of white bread and went into the scullery, out the back door and into the shed. I left the shed door slightly open behind me, so I could see where Kevin had put the pup. The shed was where Dad stored turf, coal and chopped logs to be burned during winter. There was always a dusty old smell in here — especially now, in the summer. But the good thing about keeping the pup in this shed was that Dad wasn't likely to come in here: any tools that he might be looking for, saws and hammers and shovels, were in the smaller shed beside this one. The only problem was that, if Dad went into the tool shed, he might hear the pup whimpering — which she was doing now.

I went over to the box, got down on my hunkers and tried to feed her some bread soaked in milk. She took it no problem. I held her for a while, stroking her velvety back, and then I kissed her gently on the top of her head and put her back into the box. I petted her a few more times and she licked my finger.

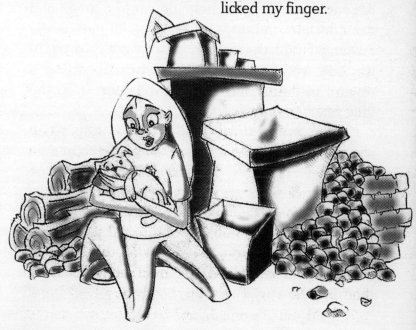

Tears sprang into my eyes, I felt so sorry for those other pups. Then I got angry with Johnny Mac again. I just wished there was a way to make him pay for what he did to those poor pups, and for what he nearly did to this one. If I had had poison, I would have put it in the scones that Mam made for him – just enough to make him sick for a week; and then, when he came back a week later, I could poison him again for another week. I would keep on doing that, so it would take yonks for him to die.

I went out to check on the pup twice more that evening, to make sure she was okay. I had no difficulty getting back out; neither Mam nor Dad, nor Ruthie, for that matter, suspected a thing. It was just as well, because I wouldn't have wanted to be depending on Kevin to help: he got in a mood and went upstairs and stayed in his room for most of the evening. I think the fact that there were no drugs in the bag, which meant that he wasn't getting a reward or getting his dial in the paper or on the telly, had him on a downer.

He didn't come down until Mam went up, when she was putting Ruthie to bed, and asked him if he wanted a cup of tea and some biscuits. Then he came into the living-room, where me and Dad were sitting watching Clint Eastwood shooting holes in everyone for a few dollars, and said, "Would you like a cup of tea, Uncle Joseph?"

"No thanks, son," Dad said, treating me to a look that said: *Now why can't you be like St Kevin?*

"Would you like one, Mary?"

After I got over the shock, I turned round and stared at Kevin, and he jerked his head sideways for me to come out to the kitchen.

"No, it's all right, I'll get it myself," I said, and left the room to the sound of Dad drooling about how wonderful Kevin was.

"Hey, Mary, will you come up to the cabin with me tomorrow?" Kevin said, when we got into the kitchen.

"What do you want to go back there for?"

"I was just thinking that there might be another bag hidden somewhere."

"A third bag?"

"Yeah," he said, excitement coming back into his eyes.

"But wouldn't that belong to the little boy who lives down the lane?" I said.

"What little boy?"

"You know, the boy in 'Baa baa black sheep'."

"Ah, you're a lula," Kevin said, disgusted.

"Maybe, but I am not going up to that cabin to look for any more black bags. That place gives me the creeps," I said, filling the kettle.

Kevin sighed, looked down at the floor for a minute, and then grabbed my arm and said, "Well, will you come if I give you three euro?"

"Five," I said, playing him at his own game – a game that I was starting to enjoy. "And I want the money now."

"I'll give it to you along with the tenner that I'm getting off me ma," the worm said, trying to wriggle his way out of paying me.

"You'll give it to me now, or else you can go up to the cabin on your own." I flashed him a Hollywood smile.

"All right," he said. His face actually turned pale as he stuck his hand into his pocket. You would swear I was Count Dracula about to drain his life's blood from him. He held the coins that Dad had given him in his hand and started running the fingers of his other hand over them and gazing at them with a long sad face. In fact, his face was so sad and his eyes so tearful that I almost told him to keep the five euro — almost, but I didn't.

"Come on, Kevin, hand it over. I don't want to be here all night."

Reluctantly, he stretched out his hand. I took the money, thanked him and smiled. Still smiling, I poured the boiling water from the kettle into the teapot.

"What yeh smiling at?" Kevin said.

"Oh, nothing," I said, though I was tempted to tell him that, while I was watching the telly, I had been thinking about going back up to the cabin again; there was definitely something weird going on up there. But I couldn't tell that to Kevin, just in case he freaked. At the same time, I couldn't resist saying to him, "Cousin Kevin, will I pour you a nice cup of tea?" just to get him going.

"No!" he said. "I don't want any tea from a basket case." He charged up the stairs, with his cheeks flaming red with temper. I laughed, poured myself a cup of tea and ate a chocolate biscuit. They had never tasted better.

Chapter Ten

The next morning, I got up soon after I heard Mam going out the door on her way to eight o'clock Mass. I dressed, went downstairs and put some milk and bread into a small bowl; I was about to go out the back and feed the pup when Kevin, the doughnut, came charging down the stairs.

"When are we going to the cabin?" he said, ready for action.

"We won't be going anywhere till we've had breakfast, and we've got to go to Mass," I said, heading out to the shed.

"What time is Mass?" he said, following me.

"Second Mass isn't till eleven."

"What! There's no other Mass?"

"We only have two, eight o'clock and eleven o'clock, and we've missed the first one."

"Oh, no! This is the pits," Kevin said, shaking his head.

"What are you moaning about? It's better for us to go to eleven o'clock Mass, because we can go straight to the cabin afterwards on our own. Dad will bring Ruthie to the shop with him to get the Sunday papers, like he always does."

"It's still the pits having to wait," Kevin said, pulling a long face.

"Well, there's nothing we can do about it, so that's tough — you'll just have to wait."

Kevin's face got longer — but not as long as it got when we came out from Mass and Dad said, "Mary, you and Kevin take Ruth home; I have to go and see someone. I'll be back in a few hours."

"Oh, no!" Kevin let a big groan out of him.

"Don't worry, Kevin," Dad said. "I have a surprise for you all when I come back. I'm taking ye to Bellackey stud farm, and Kevin, you'll get to ride around on a thoroughbred horse instead of an old donkey. So make sure you're ready to go at three o'clock sharp. This man I'm going to see will drive us there." And Dad walked off. He hadn't gone very far when Ruthie ran after him to give him a kiss.

"You said your da always takes Ruthie with him!" Kevin said, turning on me.

"Don't start, Kevin. I didn't know he was going to do this, so don't blame me."

"Now we'll have to bring her home before we go to the cabin," Kevin said, in a real whinging voice.

"No, we can't do that. We'll have to bring her to the cabin with us."

"No way!" Kevin said, shaking his head wildly. "We're not bringing her and her stupid doll."

"Then we won't be going to the cabin."

"Why not? Can't we dump her back at the house and then go?" Kevin said, his face red with temper.

"Because we won't have time, not if we're going to be back at the house in time to go with Dad to

Bellackey stud farm so as you can play at being a cowboy."

"Then I won't go to Bellackey."

"Yeah, right. Well, you better go after Dad and tell him that, because if he comes back at three and we're not there he'll go ape."

Kevin began shuffling from one foot to the other and shaking his shoulders. I thought he was going to start break-dancing, the way he was going on.

"All right, we'll bring her with us," he finally said, sighing dejectedly.

We went a shorter way to the cabin, which was just as well, because I spent a lot of time walking back to pick up Lulu. Ruthie kept dropping the doll and wouldn't let me carry it, so in the end I had to carry her and the doll or we would never have got to the cabin.

As if this wasn't bad enough, I had to listen to Kevin burning the ears off me as well. "I told you, you should have brought her home first."

"Well, I didn't, so shut up being a pain. Okay?" I said. I was getting touchy from carrying Ruthie. The heat wasn't helping things, either; even though the day was cloudy, it was still very warm. As I walked through the woods, I could feel my back getting sticky with sweat. The air in the woods felt heavy and hot, and even the woods seemed to be a bit on the dozy side: there were few birds twittering, though there was the faint sound of a dog barking every so often.

The sharp barking became more noticeable as we got nearer to the cabin. And there was another sound — a sort of hoarse growling.

"What's that?" Kevin said, looking at me wide-eyed.

"It must be another dog."

"Sure sounds funny for a dog." He started swaying back and forth, all excited. "I'm going to find out."

"No! Kevin, wait. Don't go charging up there," I said, but he just legged it.

I started to get a funny feeling in my stomach about this, a feeling that was telling me to turn around and forget about going to the cabin. The feeling grew stronger when Kevin came tearing back, with his eyes popping, and grabbed my arm. "Mary! Mary! You have to come and see this," he whispered.

"See what? Tell me!" I said, the feeling in my stomach reaching up and giving my heart a thump.

"C'mon." He started dragging me with him.

"Where are we going?" Ruthie said, in an almost-crying voice. "I want to go home."

"We'll go home in a minute, Ruthie, just as soon as we see what's up here," I said, more to reassure myself than anything else.

"But I want to . . ." She whispered something into my ear, but I couldn't hear what she was on about, above the noise that my heart was making and the horrible hoarse growling sound that was coming from the direction of the cabin.

"Get down!" Kevin said, when we reached the spot that looked down on the cabin.

"What is it?" I said, as we crouched down in the covering of green ferns.

"Take a look for yourself," Kevin said, panting. "But make sure they don't see you."

I got up slowly, the ferns tickling my face as I rose, and peeped down at the cabin. There was nothing happening there, but there definitely was something going on further over, where the square pit was. I could see a group of men huddled about the pit, murmuring as they looked down into it. One of the men was Johnny Mac, and in between looking down into the pit he was swigging from a bottle.

I went to get up a bit more, to try to see what they were all gawking at, but Ruthie pulled me back down. "I have to go *now*," she whispered into my ear again.

"Oh, okay!" I said, copping on to what she was on about. "Just go behind one of those trees down there and no one will see you. We'll wait here for you, but don't be long." I was dying to take another look at what was going on down below.

As Ruthie went off to do her business, I took another look down at the men. There were about eight of them standing around the pit; some of them were drinking from cans, while others were swigging from bottles. Then a few of them started shouting, "Go on! Go on!" to whatever was in the pit.

"What are they doing?" Kevin hissed.

"I can't see." I was dying to stand up fully, but I was afraid that one of the men below might turn around and we'd all be sussed.

Down below, there was a sharp yelping sound, and then the men started cursing and stood back from the pit; I saw then that it was covered over with a layer of chicken wire. One of the men knelt down, rolled back a corner of the wire, and leaned over into the pit. As he did, the temptation to stand all the way up became too much. I got up on my tippy-toes and stretched my neck as much as I could, and watched the man below. But, just as his hand was coming back out of the pit, Kevin dragged me down to the ground.

"I think one of them saw us," he said. His voice sounded like it was being rubbed with sandpaper.

"Are you sure?"

"Yeah!" Kevin nodded his head rapidly.

"Well then, we better get out of here fast."

"Okay," Kevin said. He was about to take off when I grabbed him.

"Where's Ruthie?"

"I don't know; you're the one that told her to go down there behind one of the trees."

I ran down and called her name, as loud as I dared. There was no answer. Then, suddenly, she came out from behind a tree, and my heart nearly stopped. There was a man with her, and he had a hold of her hand. It was the tall thin man in the grey suit who had been talking to Johnny Mac in the field yesterday.

"You two better come over here as well," he said, staring at us with stone-cold black eyes from beneath a grey chequered cap. I could see out of the corner of my eye that Kevin was trying to edge away. "And don't think about making a run for it, sonny, because this fellow will have your leg for lunch before you can break into a gallop."

He flicked the leash that he held in his other hand, and a sleeky black pit bull made a run at us with bared teeth. The man's wizened face cracked into a brown-toothed smile. He choked back the dog and started talking to it: "Easy, precious, save your strength. . . ." When he spoke there was a huge lump in the front of his neck that kept going up and down. His neck reminded me of the neck of one of the turkeys that the butcher in the village hangs up at Christmastime: red and scrawny.

"Please, Mister, let my sister go. We have to get home," I said in a tearful voice, as my heart got over the shock and started beating again.

"Yeah, our da will be out looking for us all over the place if we don't go now," Kevin added, getting in on the act.

"Oh, don't worry, I won't keep ye too long. Soon as we finish up at the cabin, ye can all go on your merry way. Can't let ye go running off and bringing half the countryside up here to stick their noses in where they're not wanted, now can I?" he said, in a menacing voice.

"We would never do that," I said. Kevin joined in with "We swear we wouldn't," and drew two huge Xs across his chest with his finger.

"Ye can swear all ye want, but the only place ye're going is to the cabin. Now come over here and grab hold of your little sister's hand," he said gruffly. "And get moving!"

Chapter Eleven

I went over to Ruthie. She jumped up into my arms and refused to get down, so I had to carry her. When we got near the cabin, the thin man shouted over to the other men standing around the pit, and they bunched closer together and turned their faces away so as we couldn't get a good look at them or see what was going on in the pit. But I did catch a glimpse of a white-faced animal with two black stripes down its face, and I knew then what was going on.

Badger-baiting. I didn't know whether to cry or get sick, I felt so bad when I thought of the poor badger being torn to pieces by a dog and all those men just watching and letting it happen. Sickos, the lot of them.

As we got to the cabin, I kept looking over at the huddle of men, trying to see if I could recognise any of them. There was one I knew, even though he had his head bowed and his back to me; I would have recognised him even if it was dark and I was wearing a blindfold.

"In ye go," the thin man said, opening the cabin door. As we went inside, Johnny Mac staggered over after us and started staring us out of it – or staring Kevin out of it, more like. Kevin kept his head down and pressed closer to me. Johnny Mac stood for a while, just nodding his head and grunting out of him. The stench of alcohol, mingled with the other smells coming from him and from the cabin, would have made a dung beetle get sick.

"We'll leave them in here till we're finished," the thin man said. "You stay here, Johnny, while I go and get Caesar to keep an eye on them. I'll not be a second."

"Take your time, Martin," Johnny Mac said, still staring at Kevin, whose head was now nearly down at his ankles.

"Nothing to say for yourself?" Johnny Mac said, when Martin left. "What's wrong, is your tongue stuck?" He moved right over beside us. Dad was right: Johnny Mac did have a left eye. I could see it, or at least I saw something that looked a bit like a shiny piece of an eye and a bit like the silvery path that a snail leaves on the ground. "What was that you said?" Johnny Mac smiled and wet his lips, like he was about to have a bowl of strawberries and cream sprinkled with loads of chocolate flakes.

Kevin hadn't said a word, hadn't even taken a breath; he was standing beside me like a statue. Johnny Mac moved even closer, so close that when he said, "Well, let's just see if I can help loosen that tongue of yours for you," some flecks of spit hit me on the side of the face.

Johnny Mac reached out a grubby hand, grabbed a hold of Kevin's ear and twisted it. Kevin roared, and Ruthie buried her head deeper into my neck.

"Ah, it speaks," Johnny Mac said, the smile turning the corners of his mouth upwards. "It speaks." He twisted Kevin's ear again, and as Kevin let another roar out of him, Johnny Mac closed his good eye and let the smile fill his face.

Suddenly the door swung open and Martin came in with a pit bull on a leash. The dog was bleeding from cuts over its left eye and around its mouth and from long red scratches in its brindled coat.

"Come on, Johnny, let's get this thing over with before somebody else comes. The lads are getting very uneasy out there."

Johnny Mac gave Kevin's ear one more twist and staggered out of the cabin. Martin tied the dog's leash to one of the legs of the table; he looked over at us and said, "If any of ye move, Caesar here will savage ye." He stood up, took a small bottle of whiskey out of his pocket and had a swallow of it. Then he walked out of the cabin and shut the door.

I kept my eyes glued to the dog as it stood there with blood dripping from the corner of its mouth onto the floor. The sound of its panting filled the cabin. I kept telling myself that everything would be all right once we did nothing to upset the dog, that whatever was going on outside in the pit would soon be over and then we could all go home. I had myself almost convinced of this when things started to go wrong, horribly wrong.

First, Ruthie lifted her head to see what was happening, saw the state of the dog, and promptly buried her head back in my neck — but not before she plastered Lulu against the side of my face. I was afraid to lift my hand to move Lulu in case the dog went spare. Then Kevin, the weasel, decided to inch away from us. Immediately the dog growled, low and threatening, and moved towards us as far as the leash would allow, which was much, much too far for my liking.

"Kevin. What are you doing?" I whispered, staring at the leg of the table where Martin had knotted the leash. The knot didn't seem to be tied all that tightly, and the table looked like it was ready to collapse. My knees began trembling.

"Kevin –" I turned my head slightly, and one of Lulu's arms ended up spread across my lips and nearly went into my mouth. I turned my head a little bit more and copped what Kevin was at. The door had swung open invitingly – Martin hadn't bothered to tie it shut properly – and Kevin was trying to slide his way over to it.

He took another step and the dog went ballistic, snarling and jumping against the leash. "Oh, Mammy!" Kevin cried, as he legged it back and tried to burrow his way in behind me.

The dog kept on snarling and jumping. It was getting nowhere at first, but then the table began to groan and tilt forward, letting the dog nearer to us – or to me; Kevin was buried in behind me. "Kevin, will you stop pushing me towards the dog!" I tried to say, but I couldn't with Lulu pressed against my mouth. I glanced at the table. It was still moving. In another few seconds it would be on the floor. My whole body began to shake.

The dog made another jump and snapped at my leg. It just missed me; my jeans were spattered with the blood from its mouth. I gasped with fright, and Lulu's arm went into my mouth and smacked off my tonsils. Instinctively, I put my hand up and pulled it out of my gob. As I did, the dog jumped up and snapped at Lulu.

I threw Lulu onto the floor and immediately the dog was all over her, its teeth digging into poor Lulu's head. Now was our chance. I belted for the door. Somehow, Kevin got there before me and was out and running towards the trees before I was even out of the cabin.

Luckily for us, the men were too taken up with what was going on in the pit to notice us disappearing into the woods. I ran as fast as I could, but the weight of Ruthie slowed me down. I tried to get her to run beside me, but there was no way she would take her arms from around my neck. So I kept running, feeling that my lungs were going to burst at any minute. Once I thought I heard someone shouting behind us in the distance, but I didn't dare turn around.

As if this wasn't bad enough, Kevin, whom I could still see darting amongst the trees up ahead, was going off in the wrong direction. I prayed that he would slow down or at least turn around, so as I could wave to him; but no, he just kept galloping on, getting himself lost. I tried to call him, but my throat was too dry and the words got stuck. Eventually I managed to shriek out his name. He turned, twisting his head in every direction before he saw us. I pointed for him to head the other way, down to the right, and as soon as he sussed what I was on about he took off.

I went to run again, but I couldn't. My legs felt dead and my arms were killing me; drops of sweat the size of golf balls were rolling down my face, stinging my eyes, and my back felt like someone had turned a hosepipe on it. So I started walking as fast as I could. I tried again to coax Ruthie to get down and walk, by telling her that everything was all right now, that we were nearly home; but she still wouldn't move. She was stuck to me like a tattoo.

I walked on, taking the occasional look behind to make sure that we weren't being followed. We weren't. I began to breathe easier, and even Ruthie took a chance and came up for air from the hollow in my neck.

I was just picking my way down an area of the woods that was littered with turned-up roots and trees that had been blown over during last winter's storms, when Ruthie started jumping about in my arms and whimpering out of her like a pup. I looked back and couldn't believe what I saw. The thin man, Martin, was coming after us. And, though he was a long way behind us, he definitely had spotted us: he suddenly started running — running in our direction.

I begged Ruthie to get down and run, I told her I would hold on to her hand, but all she did was shake her head before burying it in my neck and wrapping her arms and her legs around me even more tightly than before. My body began to shake as panic set in again. What could I do? I couldn't outrun him — not while I was carrying Ruthie.

I thought about hiding behind a tree, but the trees looked too skinny to conceal the two of us. I knew that, a little bit further down the wood, the ground was covered with ferns; we would be able to hide among them. I looked back at Martin; he was getting closer. It was useless. We would never make it to the ferns before he caught up on us. We would have to hide behind a tree, and we would have to do it now.

I looked around for a thick one; and then I noticed that under some of the uprooted trees there were fairly deep holes, like little caves. I sneaked into the deepest one I could find and prayed.

It took about a minute, the longest minute in my whole life, for Martin to come near to where we were hiding. I could just about hear his dull footsteps tramping about — and then the footsteps stopped.

I held my breath. Drops of sweat ran down from my forehead and some of them ended up gathering on the tip of my nose, tickling the life out of me. I was about to rub them with my hand when I heard footsteps again — and they were getting closer.

Ruthie let loose a low sob, and I was sure that we were sussed. Martin had to have heard her. But he hadn't: he was loudly gulping from a bottle. I pressed my hand lightly over Ruthie's mouth, in case she sobbed again.

"Where did they get to?" I heard Martin say, his voice full of frustration. He took another few steps. Now he was right over us. I closed my eyes and begged God to make him go away.

God must have heard my prayers, because Martin suddenly said, "I've had enough of this," and started to walk away. Me and Ruthie were safe — or, at least, we would have been, if Ruthie hadn't started making a rasping sound, like the one she was making after Snooper got knocked down.

"Come on out. I can hear ye."

Trembling, I moved out into the open.

Martin was only a few feet away, standing on top of another upturned tree-root with a smug grin on his face. "Where's the little boyo hiding?"

I didn't answer; I couldn't, because I was crying. "Well, let's see now . . . where could the little ferret be?" Martin said, looking about.

I took a few steps back, but he copped immediately. "And where do you think you're going?" There was an angry look in Martin's eyes and on his tightly drawn lips. "I've had enough of ye and your carry-on." He took a step towards us; and as he did, his foot sank in the spongy grass that was growing around the top of the root. He fell flat on his face.

I went to make a run for it, but I had only gone a few steps when his words stuck me to the ground. "Stay where you are!"

I turned. Martin was getting to his feet. "I'll teach ye to do what you're told," he said, with fire in his eyes.

"Oh, please don't touch us," I begged, tears pouring down my face. Ruthie was bawling as well.

Martin took a step towards us, roared and clapped his hand on his right ankle. I moved back a bit. "You're going nowhere," he shouted, standing upright; he took another step towards us, roared, and grabbed his ankle again.

I turned and, with my heart feeling like it was going to explode, ran as fast as the weight of Ruthie in my arms would let me. As I ran, I had a terrible feeling that, at any second, a hand was going to grab me. I wanted to stop and look around to see where Martin was, but I was too scared.

Eventually, I had to stop: I was no longer able to force air into my lungs or get my legs to move. I looked round, but I couldn't see him, which for a second made me feel worse. And then I heard him, cursing and swearing, a fair way behind us; and at last I caught a glimpse of him hobbling back in the direction of the cabin.

"It's all right, Ruthie. It really is. Look, he's going the other way." I managed to squeeze the words out past my gasping breath. Ruthie's breathing seemed to ease when she heard that; but, though she poked her head up to have a look at Martin, there was no way she would get down and walk for me. Totally wrecked, I walked on – or maybe I should say staggered on – barely able to see through the river of sweat that was flowing down my forehead into my eyes.

Chapter Twelve

We were halfway down the field when we saw Dad, Mam, Kevin and Mr Stevens — our neighbour, who must have driven them — push open the gate and race towards us. Dad grabbed Ruthie, who was all right but still wheezing a bit. "Are you okay?" he almost shouted at me.

I nodded and started to cry with relief. Dad gave Ruthie to Mam, and then he wrapped his arms around me and hugged me.

A few seconds later, a car screeched to a halt down on the road and two gardaí came running up to us; one of them was Tom Flanagan, who lived near us.

"What's going on, Mary?" Tom said.

"They're badger-baiting up at the cabin, and — and —" I stuttered, tears making me lose my voice.

"Johnny Mac and a man named Martin held us prisoners," Kevin said, jumping in. "And his dog nearly savaged us to death, and then Martin came after us himself."

"He can hardly walk because he twisted his ankle," I said, finding my voice.

"Where's the cabin?" Tom said.

"I'll show you," Dad said, and he, Tom, Mr Stevens and the other garda went running off into the woods.

Kevin wanted to go with them; but Mam, who was holding Ruthie and rubbing her back, said, "No, Kevin, I think what we'll do is go home."

Mam carried Ruthie home, which was just as well, because I was completely burned out. Kevin and I walked beside her, and all the way to the house there wasn't a word out of either of us. There wasn't even a word out of Mam. It was like we were all walking behind an imaginary coffin, and the sound of Ruthie whinging every so often in Mam's arms just added to that feeling.

I was sort of half-expecting to get an earful from Mam about bringing Ruthie and Golden Boy up to the cabin in the first place, and, to tell the truth, I would have preferred her to let rip at me as we walked home, because at that point I was too wasted to mind. But she didn't. I think she was just glad to see that we were all okay – though, by the time our little procession reached the house, I noticed that Mam was throwing some loaded looks in my direction. The inquisition was on the way.

As soon as I got in, I went straight upstairs and had a bath. I put half a gallon of bubble bath in the water and just soaked my bones. Mam and her inquisition would have to wait. Anyway, I figured, as I felt the water soothe the bod, Mam wouldn't be too bad – she'd go on a bit, but I mean, what's new about that? – but Dad would be a different story. He would just go on and on and on. I felt like sticking my head under the water and not coming up.

By the time I eventually went back downstairs, Kevin had obviously told Mam most of what had happened, which was a gift for me. There was no way she would ever give out to the Chosen One, though she was making a lot of *tch-tch* sounds that got a lot louder when she saw me. And then, as I went over to the sink to get a drink of water, she turned to me and said, "Mary, what put that idea into your head, to go up to the cabin after Johnny Mac?"

"*My* idea?" I said, and immediately Kevin was out the back door.

"Yes, your idea." Mam shook her head. "I just hope that you realise now how foolish and dangerous that was, and that you'll never do anything like that ever again." From the sound of her voice, I was in for a lengthy lecture.

But before she could say any more, Kevin came back in, holding the pup in his hands, and Mam's heart melted. Ruthie got all excited and started screaming, "Let me hold her! Let me hold her!"

"Isn't she absolutely gorgeous! Where did you get her?" Mam said, stroking the pup with her fingertips.

"I found her; she was. . . ." Kevin told Mam the whole story – and what a story. No one figured in it except, of course, himself.

"Weren't you a very lucky little puppy to survive all that!" Mam kept saying, when Kevin had finished his fairy tale. The one good thing about the fairy tale was that it really softened Mam up – so much that when Ruthie said, "Mammy, Mammy, can we keep her?" Mam shook her head at first but eventually said yes. Oh, and there was another good thing: Mam gave me no more grief, especially after everyone agreed to call the new member of the family "Lucky".

Now all I had to worry about was the ear-bashing I'd get from Dad when he got home. I don't know what time he did get home, because after I had my dinner I went up to my room to have a rest, and fell asleep.

At eleven o'clock the next morning, I managed to crawl out of bed. My legs were stiff and my arms were hanging off me. I dressed and went to the bathroom, dreading the thought of what was to come. I just hoped that Dad would wait till after breakfast before he began the litany; I wouldn't be able to take him moaning into my face on an empty stomach.

As I started to go downstairs, I could hear voices below – strange voices. At first I thought I was hearing things, but when I went down a few steps, I clearly heard someone say: "And how did you and Mary and Ruth finally manage to get out of the cabin?"

"Well, I sort of grabbed the doll and flung it on the floor, 'cause I knew the dog would dive on it."

"Good thinking. And that gave you the time to get out of the cabin?"

"Yeah," Kevin said. "I knew it would; that's why I did it."

I couldn't believe what Kevin, the filthy, rotten little liar, was saying.

"That was very, very clever, Kevin," whoever-it-was said. "And what did you do then?"

This was just too much; there was no way I was letting Kevin away with this. I dashed downstairs and ended up being nearly blinded by a flashing light. Someone was taking photographs. Before I got my sight back, I was grabbed and made stand beside Kevin. Ruthie was lifted into my arms, and the whole room became alive with flashes. Then someone shouted that the television crew was here, and someone else rushed Kevin outside to be interviewed.

For the next hour, the outside of the house was buzzing with people. Dad's boss, Mr Bailey – a small fat man who looks like Danny DeVito, with a black curly head of hair — was there and was interviewed, and so was the Minister who looks after the forests. Then, when the television crew and the newspaper reporters went away, Mr Bailey came in and said: "Joe, I've been talking to the Minister about this gruesome carry-on up at the cabin, and I've also been telling him what the neighbours have been saying to me about seeing some right unsavoury-looking characters wandering about the woods. The Minister is more than concerned; he hopes to encourage people from Pebblestown to come out walking in the woods, as part of a Get Fit campaign." Mr Bailey blew air through his chubby lips and threw his eyes up to the ceiling. "Anyway, to cut to the quick of the matter, the Minister has suggested that we have someone patrolling the woods, like a forest ranger, so that this barbaric business of setting dogs against badgers never happens again. Having a forest ranger would certainly act as a deterrent to these sick-minded individuals. He asked me if I could think of anyone suitable for the job. I thought about you, and the trouble you're having with your ould ticker; and, since there's no one who knows these woods better than your good self, what do you say?"

Dad raced over, shook Mr Bailey's hand and hugged him. I thought for a few moments that he was going to kiss him, which would have been totally gross, but he kissed me and Ruthie and Mam and Kevin instead. Then Dad took out a bottle of whiskey and poured Mr Bailey a drink. Mam had a glass of sherry; the rest of us were given lemonade and promises. I think Dad would have had a party, only Mr Bailey said he had to go.

Shortly after he left, Garda Tom Flanagan called and asked Kevin and me if we would be able to identify or give a description of any of the men we'd seen up at the cabin. Kevin and I both told him that all we had seen of the men were their backs.

"That's a pity," Tom said, flicking his fingers through his short brown hair. "Still, we caught that fella Martin, and Mr Johnny Mac; he was too drunk to try to get away. The others, I'm afraid, scattered and scrammed like rats down a sewer."

"I hope Johnny Mac will be prosecuted for this," Dad said.

"You can depend on it," Tom said. "He might get a spell in jail, with a bit of luck. One thing's for sure: he won't be keeping dogs, or breeding them, ever again."

"What did he kill the pups for?" I said. Tom mentioning about dogs was making me think of the pups we'd found.

"Yeah, why didn't he sell them?" Kevin added. Just like him to be thinking of money.

Before Tom could answer, Mam stood up and said she was bringing Ruthie up for a lie-down. But I copped that it was Mam who wanted to lie down: the sherry had gone to her head.

"He only killed the female pups," Tom said. "They wouldn't be as aggressive nor as vicious as the male ones. He wouldn't bother selling them, wouldn't even give them away, the. . . ." Tom paused and sighed. "Anyway," he went on, "he buried them all up at the cabin, along with anything else that he wanted to bury; the cabin was his dumping ground."

"Those poor pups," I said, my voice beginning to shake. "How can anyone be so cruel to animals?"

"He should be shot," Kevin said.

"Flogged would be better," Tom said. "But no matter; I'll be keeping a very tight watch on Mr Johnny Mac from now on."

I started to feel a lot better after I heard Tom say that.

About an hour after Tom left, Aunt Eileen arrived and was told the whole story.

"I knew it, I just knew it," she said, smacking her red lips together. "I knew there was something nasty about that beastly-looking creature." She sat down and began waving her hand in front of her face. "Oh, I feel faint after hearing that."

Then she grabbed hold of Kevin and squeezed him to her chest. "My son the hero," she said, leaving lipstick tracks on his hair. "Tell Mammy again how brave you were up in that cabin."

Kevin turned and looked at me, and then whispered into his mother's ear. "He wants to give Mary some money so as she can buy a poster," Aunt Eileen said, picking her handbag up off the floor.

"Ah, now there's a thoughtful lad for you, if ever there was one," Dad said.

I thanked Kevin for the money and then went outside to check on Lucky before I threw up. A little while later, Kevin followed me out with a big grin across his face.

"Look what I got from your da," he said, waving a ten-euro note in front of my face. "And I got five euro from your ma." He began hee-hee-ing out of him.

I felt like crying; there was no winning with him. I was about to tell him to go away and not be annoying me, when I looked up the hill and thought of something.

"That doesn't matter," I said as I shut the shed door. "Because, Kevin," I sighed, "there's just no way I can beat you. I'm just glad you gave me the money for the poster. Thanks." Kevin looked at me as if I had three heads.

"And if you want to have a ride on Jaws or Slug before you go, I'll help you to get on their backs." Kevin's mouth became one giant O of disbelief. "But maybe you don't feel like it now," I said, heading towards the house.

"Yeah, I do. I do!" Kevin called after me, shaking with excitement.

"Okay, but we better hurry in case Dad or your mam comes out."

Kevin was up the hill, over the fence and standing beside Jaws and Slug before I had gone past the shed.

"We'll try Jaws first," I said. I made Kevin put his left hand on Jaws's neck. "Now bend down a bit and lift your right foot." I put my hands under his foot. "Now, on the count of three, you jump as high as you can and I'll push you up. One, two, aaaand —"

Kevin let a deafening roar out of him and was off over the fence and running down the hill, his right hand gripping his backside, before I had a chance to say "three" — which was just as well, because Aunt Eileen had just come out the back door and was calling him.

When I stopped laughing, I went down to the house. Everyone was out the front, so I went out to say goodbye.

"Are you sure you won't stay for tea, Eileen?" Mam said into the window of Aunt Eileen's car.

"Not at all; I want to get home and inform the neighbours that my son will be on the six o'clock news. I don't want them missing that." Then she gave Kevin a clatter on the back of the head. "Will you sit easy, you born fidget!"

"Bye-bye, Kevin," I said, tapping on his side window and smiling. "Have a comfortable trip."

Kevin turned and glared at me, his dial red with anger, and then he hopped about in the seat again – still feeling the effect of Jaws's teeth, no doubt.

"Will you stop jumping around like a kangaroo so as I can drive!" Aunt Eileen gave Kevin another clatter, and then she kissed him on the side of the head and called him her little hero before she sped off down the road.

As I went back into the house with Dad, I started thinking about what had been going on up in the woods. "Why do you think Johnny Mac and those men were making the dogs fight the badgers?" I said to Dad.

"It's hard to know what makes people do such cruel things. Not even Solomon himself would be able to figure that one out. I suppose all you can say is that there's something seriously wrong, something lacking, in people who would do that." He heaved his shoulders and sighed. Then, as we got into the house, he paused for a moment and took a deep breath.

"But do you know, Mary," he said real loud, so as Mam, who was over at the sink filling the kettle, would hear, "I reckon that in Johnny Mac's case those scones your mother was feeding him might just have affected his mind in some way."

"Joseph O'Neill, how dare you say such a thing!" Mam said, grabbing a tea towel from the draining board and belting him with it. Dad just laughed. He was definitely back to his old self, and I was definitely over the worst year of my life – so far.